CURRENCY

REVISED SECOND EDITION

CURRENCY

REVISED SECOND EDITION

L TODD WOOD

LIBERTY ISLAND
LET YOUR RIGHT BRAIN RUN FREE

A LIBERTY ISLAND BOOK
ISBN: 978-1-94794-213-4
ISBN (eBook): 978-1-94794-214-1

Currency:
A Financial Thriller
© 2018 by L Todd Wood
All Rights Reserved

Cover design by Matt Margolis

Liberty Island
libertyislandmag.com

Published in the United States of America

To Olga,
Who believed in me

To Larry and Helen,
Who kept me going

And to my friend Joanne,
Who showed me the way

"It is better to be feared than loved."

—Niccolò Machiavelli, The Prince

PROLOGUE

Weehawken, New Jersey
July 11, 1804

The smartly dressed, older man came first, sitting erect and still as death in the rear of the long oar boat as it silently rowed across the wide river. The moon cast an eerie glow across the fast-moving, silky, black current.

He was balding, middle-aged, and had dark features. However, he was in a much darker mood, a murderous mood in fact. He was the kind of man who never forgot anything, especially the stain on his honor. His eyes bored holes in the back of the man sitting in front of him, and he did not notice his surroundings, as his mind was lost in thought. He was there to right a wrong he had suffered.

To this end he was joined by two other men seated near him, as well as two additional young rowers and his dueling second at the head of the craft, a total of five. The only sound was the water lapping like a running brook as the oars slipped in and out of the calm, silvery surface. Slowly the boat crossed the dark current. Preoccupied, the passenger did not hear. He was focused only on the task ahead of him.

They beached the long oar boat on the bank, and he and the three men quickly scurried into the woods as the rowers stayed behind. Immediately the four gentlemen began to clear the brush along the ledge facing the water. The birds awoke but no one heard. Their singing cast an odd, joyful sound, contrasting eerily with the morbid events unfolding beneath them.

A blond man younger by a year arrived a half hour later in a similar craft with a smaller entourage. He was a person of importance and seemed rather arrogant. In fact, he had a brilliant mind. Unfortunately he had a habit of taunting others with his brilliance, which is what brought him to where he was at this hour. His pompous mood seemed out of touch with the somber circumstances.

One of his party was a well-respected physician. His second, sitting in the bow, carried an ornate box the size of a breadbasket. Inside were two Wogdon dueling pistols, the finest in the world at the time. The pair of weapons had already claimed the lives of a handful of men. One of those killed had been the younger man's son.

The first party made themselves known, and the group who had just arrived made their way up the embankment to join them. Salutations were exchanged.

The seconds set marks on the ground for the two men ten paces from each other. The younger man, since challenged, had the option of choosing his spot and had already selected to be facing the river. The two antagonists loaded their pistols in front of the witnesses, which was the custom, and the seconds walked into the woods and turned their backs. This way they would not be party to the scene and could not be charged with a crime, as dueling was now illegal. The honorable gentleman was becoming a rare breed. Times were changing.

The blond man's second began counting down. Unknown to his charge's opponent, the pistols had a secret hair-trigger firing mechanism; just a slight application of pressure would ignite the powder. This was a sleight of hand to say the least.

A loud crack rang out. A few seconds later, another. Then a cry of pain. Whether the younger man accidentally fired due to the hair trigger or intentionally wasted his shot, we will never know. Historians have debated this point ever since. His shot missed his adversary and ricocheted into the surrounding trees.

The return fire from his opponent, however, was deadly. The ball pierced his abdomen and did mortal damage to his internal organs before lodging in his spine. He collapsed to the ground.

The acrid smell of gunpowder still hung in the air as the dark-haired man walked up to him writhing on the ground. He was confident in his errand as he stood over him and methodically reloaded his pistol.

"Where is it?" he asked as he calmly packed the powder down the barrel.

The seconds stepped forward out of the brush, but the older man waved them off with his pistol. The New Jersey woods were strangely quiet; the New York lights across the river twinkled in the background, soon to be obscured by the rising sun. Its rays would soon shine a bright light on the deadly events happening below.

"Where is it?" he said again sternly but softly, pointing his re-loaded pistol at the man's head as he tried to lift it off the ground and speak. The long, highly polished brass barrel reflected the early-morning sun.

Blood poured from an open wound in the younger man's gut. Although mortally wounded and lying in the dirt, he held his hand over the opening to try and stop the flow.

"Go to Hell!" he gurgled as his mouth filled with blood.

"I probably will, but I think you will beat me there." The darker gentleman chuckled and knelt down beside him. He started going through the bleeding man's pockets. "I have heard you always carry it with you." Aaron Burr knew he didn't have much time before the surgeon and seconds gathered and pulled him off. Inside the man's blood-soaked coat, he found it.

"Ahh!" he gloated smugly. He quickly hid the pouch inside his own vest and stood.

"You will never find what you are looking for!" the wounded gentleman said in a whispering laugh. His strength was ebbing. He was going to die.

"We'll see," replied Burr.

"He's all yours!" he called to the second, and the wounded man's supporter rushed forward and tended to Alexander Hamilton.

CHAPTER ONE

June 10, 2018
Bahamas

The seawater thundered over the stern as the old fishing boat attempted to cut through the eight-foot waves, soaking everyone on board to their core. Connor Murray felt the impact in his kidneys as he held on to the ladder for dear life. The tuna tower swayed above him. His arm muscle burned as he prevented himself from being tossed into the sea from the violent movement. Salt water stung his nose. The new motor growled like a wounded bear as it strained against the onslaught.

How long can this go on? he thought.

Connor had puked twice and didn't relish a third attempt, but the nausea in his gut and throbbing in his head told him it was inevitable. The other two weekend-warrior fishermen with him on the stern were leaning over the side as he contemplated his situation. He heard them groan as they tried to empty their stomachs, but there was nothing left inside them. He was miserable.

The day had started easily enough in the predawn hours as they boarded the boat at the end of New Providence Island east of Nassau. The water was calm this early in the morning. This part of the island was protected by natural reefs. The rapid change in depth as the ocean floor rose to the island caused the ocean and the island currents to crash into each other, and protected the east end from the ocean's wrath.

He had been planning this trip for weeks with his good friend. Alex, his Bahamian business colleague, had just finished overhauling an old, thirty-two-foot pilothouse cruiser, a labor of love for two years. The boat had been refurbished from bow to stern; many a weekend night they had spent drinking beer on the deck after a day's work on the "yacht," as Alex's wife called it. Connor chuckled to himself. She was a little bit of a "wannabe."

The boat was not pretty, but she was strong. Alex had seen to that. He took very good care of her. When someone tears down and rebuilds something that intricate, it becomes part of them. The boat had become his passion. His wife didn't seem to mind; she had her yacht.

Connor had met his friend years ago when Alex was the head trader at a large hedge fund located in the tony Lyford Cay area on the west end of the island. Alex mingled with the movie stars. After trading together for several years and socializing on every trip Connor took to Nassau, they became friends and trusted one another completely. They took care of one another as they both moved firms several times over the years. Their careers flourished and their wealth grew.

This trip was a much-needed change of scenery away from the Bloomberg terminal for both of them. The constant movement of the ocean was a welcome relief from the volatility of the markets. Stress relief was critical in their business. A day or two in different surroundings did wonders for one's trading acumen. "The three-day weekend was invented for Wall Street," Alex would often say.

The sun was rising as they cruised past old Fort Montague close to East Point. He could make out the row of old British twenty-four-pound cannons lining the top barricade. The fort had held up remarkably well through the centuries, considering it was constantly exposed to the elements. The history here ran deep. Connor loved it. The islands were in his blood now. The open ocean waited for them ahead.

Today the only possible negative was the sea, as there was not a cloud in the sky. Their luck was not good.

The trip out of the channel was hellish as they crossed the churning waves. The barrier reefs produced a literal wall of water the boat had to climb, as the underwater structures halted the ocean's momentum. It was no better on the other side, but Connor knew Alex would not turn back. He had promised everyone on board some fish, and this was her maiden voyage. They all quickly decided it was too rough to make the two-hour trek to Exuma, which they had planned. Instead they would stay off Paradise Island. Connor was quietly grateful.

Later in the day, after they had landed three dolphins—a bull and two females—all mercifully decided that it was too rough to continue. Now they were making their way back to protected waters, but it wasn't easy. The waves beat the side of the boat and refused to provide a respite to the passengers and crew. The fishermen were still hugging the rail in case they had to empty their stomachs again.

Thinking he would feel better higher, Connor climbed up the ladder and leaned into the back support next to Alex. He could see a line of boats making their way into the harbor to escape the violent sea.

The tower swayed violently as Alex strained to control the craft as she muddled her way up and over the crest of the waves.

"Must have taken on some water," Alex growled. "I can feel it sloshing back and forth down below. It's hard to control this pig."

Connor wasn't listening. "Tell me the latest on our discovery," he said.

* * *

April 23, 1696

Captain William Kidd turned one last time and looked over his shoulder at the Plymouth landmass disappearing in the background. The city that produced the Pilgrims had long since lost its dominance as a critical port for the Crown. The coastal lights faded in the mist.

Kidd would not miss England. He would, however, miss his beautiful wife of five years, Sarah, and their daughter in the English colony of New York, recently acquired from the Dutch, who called it New Amsterdam. The city was on its way to becoming a cultural and economic center of North America.

Sarah was one of the wealthiest women in the New World, primarily due to her inheritance from her first husband. Already she had been twice widowed, and was only in her early twenties.

He had left them several months ago to fulfill his dreams. He would not see them again for three years. Such was the life of a sailor.

This voyage has started very badly, he thought. Maybe it was a sailor's intuition, but he had an uneasy feeling in the pit of his stomach.

He turned his attention back to the *Adventure Galley*. He had overseen her construction himself in London. She had been built in record time, so there would be leaks and other imperfections to deal with, but she would do the job. Kidd had sold his former ship, *Antigua*, in order to raise funds. The King was lusting for pirate blood and treasure. He made no secret of his haste for Kidd's voyage. The new ship would have to do.

She was a strong, thirty-four-gun privateer and would be formidable when he engaged pirates. Her design was elegant at 284 tons. Her oars would be an important capability when maneuvering against an enemy. His crew, however, was another story.

He had tried to leave England several weeks earlier with an altogether different group of men. His mission was financially speculative. The men would be paid the prize booty they could seize from legitimate pirate or French ships. Therefore he wanted men of good character who were excellent seamen. Having personally chosen each of the 150 men, he took pride in his selections.

In a hurry to depart London, he had chosen not to salute several Royal Navy vessels leaving the mouth of the Thames. It had been a mistake. This was a long-standing tradition, and not following it was a direct affront to the English Navy and the King. His men had even taunted the English yachts as they passed, showing their backsides. Hence the *Adventure Galley* was boarded, and thirty-five of her best seamen were pressed into the Royal Navy. It was another several weeks before he could get Admiral Russell to return sailors to him to fill his crew. He received back landsmen and troublemakers rather than the original able-bodied seamen.

He was now on his way to New York to fill out his crew with another eighty good men. Then he could chase pirates.

"My crew will not like to be sailing under an unlucky captain," he said aloud. Perhaps it was nothing to be worried about. "Maybe we have gotten the bad luck out of the way at the start."

He turned around and faced the bow.

The open sea helped calm his nerves.

Captain Kidd was very glad to be leaving England in command of his own powerful ship. The crew could be dealt with over time. He was a restless man.

He had desperately wanted a commission from the King to command a Royal Navy vessel, and had sailed to London from New York in late 1695 in search of this honor. He loved the sea and had been a respectable member of New York society for several years. He had used his considerable maritime skills as a merchant seaman to build his wealth. Kidd was in love with his beautiful Sarah and their young daughter of the same name, whom he adored. But his first love was the sea. He wanted adventure.

He had sailed to London with a recommendation letter to

request an audience with the King in his quest to become a Royal Navy Captain. While there, he became involved in a scheme to help the monarch with his pirate problem while making money for himself and others. Several financial benefactors backed him in building a ship and outfitting it to sail against any pirate he could find, with the booty paying the mission's expenses. The profits would be split among Kidd and the powerful English gentlemen. These included the Earl of Bellomont and other aristocrats. He'd never met the King, but he did receive a written commission to perform this duty. The King was to receive ten percent of the take.

This was a dangerous gamble, and Kidd knew he was sailing in treacherous territory. He was already at odds with the Royal Navy, who presumed it was their duty to deal with the piracy issue. It was an unlucky start indeed.

He had no friends at sea, and he suspected as much as he crossed into the Atlantic. The rewards, however, could be great and in his mind were worth the risk.

Looking out over the vast ocean, he felt at peace for the first time in many years. His wife and daughter were the furthest subjects from his mind. He was with his love at last.

CHAPTER TWO

March 8, 1806

The West Virginia snow was falling heavily and had accumulated in a blanket over the lawn of the mansion two feet deep. The trees sprang from the soft surface and reached to the snow clouds above with white-covered arms. The silence was deafening in the late evening. Aaron Burr stood in the study, looking out over the magnificent gardens, which were now covered in a winter coat. The moonlight reflected off the new-fallen snow. It seemed as though they were completely alone in the Virginia woods, but he knew the staff and guards were posted elsewhere. The clock struck eleven.

He had just finished a wonderful meal with his hosts, the Blennerhassets, in their formal dining room in the main section of the sprawling home, the grandest structure in all of America away from the East Coast. The recent stroll under the covered walkway to the study had been short but exceedingly cold. He was thankful the servants had started the fireplace hours ago, so the room was comfortably warm. The only sounds were the crackling of the embers behind him. He listened to the popping and hissing and was comforted by long-forgotten memories of the same. He momentarily was brought back to his childhood, being cuddled by his mother next to the fire. It was a pleasant memory.

The owner of the study was obviously an educated man. Musical instruments occupied the corners of the room. The walls were covered with books from floor to ceiling. What was most interesting, however, was the complete chemical laboratory opposite where he was standing, one of two in the entire American West. Blennerhasset was a man of many talents.

Burr was excited. His plan, which until recently had been just that—a plan—was now a distinct possibility.

After Hamilton's death, he was indicted for murder in New York and New Jersey. Although he was eventually acquitted, his career as a politician was over. Yet he still craved two things: money and power.

The only place he surmised he could acquire both was out west. When he actually had thought up this grand design was unknown even to him; it had been percolating in his mind for as long as he could remember. He was a very ambitious man. He had been vice president of the United States, for goodness' sake. Close but yet so far.

Burr had been spurned many times before. He harbored grievances. It had started with General Washington, who refused to acknowledge his bravery in the Revolutionary War. Then other dreams had been taken from him.

So his thoughts had turned west.

The Spanish lands in North America were very poorly managed; everyone knew that. What he desired was no less than conquering these lands during the upcoming war between the United States and Spain. Then he would install himself as king.

He had leased forty thousand acres from the Spanish government in the Bastrop lands of Texas along the Ouachita River in what is now Louisiana. There he had a force of eighty men encamped, the start of an army.

I will rule benevolently, he thought.

To this end he had been contacting prominent people who he thought could help with his quest. Harman Blennerhasset was one

8

of those individuals. Burr had appealed to his vanity and his greed. It had worked.

He was a wealthy immigrant from Ireland who controlled a large island in the Ohio River. His home was the most magnificent structure Burr had ever set foot inside. The seven-thousand-square-foot mansion contained oil paintings from Europe, silver door hardware, exquisite Oriental rugs, and alabaster chandeliers with silver chains. His estate consisted of the entire landmass of the large island surrounded by the river.

Burr surmised his host wanted more money and a little glory. He was right. Tonight's dinner had sealed the bond between them and access to the resources Blennerhasset could offer.

Of course, Burr had brought his daughter, Theodosia, to Ohio with him. She was an asset when it came to impressing moneyed interests.

He had raised her as a prodigy with strict mental discipline. Fluent in Latin, Greek, and several other languages, she could intelligently converse with anyone. She was also skilled in the arts of dancing and music. Burr had seen to her education personally since his wife had died years ago. He loved "Theo" desperately.

She was also married to Governor Alston of South Carolina. After the birth of their son in 1802, her health had become frail. Burr hoped this trip would help restore her strength. After dinner this evening, she had retired early, which allowed him to speak freely to Blennerhasset.

His host's money would help, of course, in the early days of his scheme; Burr had no resources of his own to tap. The island grounds would also be a convenient training ground for the invasion force Burr was planning. In the long run, he would need serious money, money to fund an empire.

Burr smiled. *Thanks to Alexander Hamilton, I will have this.* A noise startled him, and he was brought back to reality. Someone was walking through the covered walkway from the main house to the study. He heard the door open and saw his host walk in with a smile on his face.

"You have quite excited my wife, Colonel. It is a feat even I have not been able to accomplish in quite some time. My congratulations!"

"It is good to have such believers in my capabilities, Harman. Let me congratulate you again on these splendid surroundings."

"And your daughter, sir, she is an exquisite creature!"

"Thank you, my new friend," Burr replied.

Blennerhasset was uncorking a very nice bottle of Bordeaux his servant had retrieved from the cellar beneath the study.

"I drink to the surroundings to come! I must endeavor to learn Spanish," he quipped.

"Indeed," replied Burr as he raised his glass.

***

June 10, 2018
Bahamas
Evening

Connor parked the rental car late in the evening and walked the short distance to the British Colonial Hilton in Nassau, where he typically stayed. Nassau was very hot this summer night, and he worked up a sweat as he reached the hotel. The traffic was still heavy on Bay Street as the tourist revelers hit the bars and mingled with the locals. The scene reminded him of wolves attacking the shepherd's sheep. Many a pocket was picked as dusk descended on the pirate town.

The Hilton was built on the site of an original British fort torn down at the end of the nineteenth century. A hotel designed by Henry Flagler, who built the Breakers in Palm Beach, had replaced another military structure that burned in the 1920s. The Bahamian government then rebuilt the site, and it was taken over by Hilton in the 1990s. Hilton had preserved the colonial essence that history called for. It was a great base of operations for Connor, as it sat in the middle of his clients in Nassau, and he enjoyed working from the hotel.

The monstrous hulks of three cruise ships parked on the sea side of the building dominated the harbor and lit up the evening sky. The government had just dredged the channel to accommodate this new line of massive vessels. Their stacked decks illuminated the entire Bay Street area like a glowing sun. Even with a bad economy, the pleasure cruise business was humming.

Connor had long grown used to the ships in the background, and the sight no longer startled him. He was tired from the day's trip as he arrived at the hotel, but his mind was racing.

The doorman opened the glass door, and the welcome blast of the air conditioning hit him full force in the face. The great mural of the town's past dominated the far wall above the massive stairway to the second floor.

The history of the Bahamas and the Caribbean had always fascinated Connor. Although the Bahamas was not technically the Caribbean, he lumped them together all the same.

Most Americans had no idea of the battles that had been fought here for control of the world by the colonial powers right off their doorstep. Slavery, sugar, silver, and gold were all reasons the Spanish, French, Dutch, and English had come to blows over several centuries in the West Indies and Caribbean Sea. Although Nassau had never been invaded, many forts had been built to protect the port from foreign powers or, more often than not, pirates.

With the immense gold and silver harvests the Spanish mined from the Spanish Main came intense interest from competing powers and other groups intent on relieving them of their precious-metal burden as it was transported back to the European continent. The Caribbean islands and the Bahamas, with their vast network of isolated cays, were well suited for pirates and privateers who were determined to pillage Spanish assets as they sailed north to Madrid.

When they were not attacking foreign ships, pirates would set up encampments on the cays and gorge themselves on their newly acquired plunder. These dry spells could last for months, until another hapless victim sailed by. They loved to roast the meat of local wild pigs in thin strips to survive. This food was called "bouchon," after the French word for roasted meat. This was the origin of today's bacon. Also, since they subsisted on this ration, the pirates earned the name "buccaneers."

Locations in Jamaica and Cuba specifically became famous for their pirate cities, where the thieves could congregate between exploits and spend their ill-gotten wealth. Port Royal and Tortuga were notorious examples. Nassau was also one of those places. It was one of the last pirate refuges before the European navies were able to all but snuff out the pirate vocation in the early eighteenth century.

Men such as Edward Teach, or Blackbeard, and Captain Henry Morgan became famous during this golden age of piracy. Teach was killed by English troops, while Morgan famously died in his bed of old age and a very rich man. He considered himself a privateer, but his actions had drifted into the realm of piracy over time.

As the Spanish empire waned and its mining operations slowed, the region became famous for another commodity—sugar. The agreeable climate along with a plethora of imported African slaves made the Caribbean the perfect area to grow the cane to sweeten the cups of the numerous coffee houses across Europe. The indigenous Indian population had been decimated by disease upon the arrival of the white man and could no longer be counted on in sufficient numbers by the slave masters.

The difference between a pirate and a privateer was slight. Pirating was illegal worldwide and a scourge on trade across the globe. However, a privateer was basically a pirate sanctioned by a government. If, say, England was at war with France, the two governments would sanction and fund captains to capture and pillage ships of the opposing power. The end result was the same. People were killed or imprisoned, and ships and cargo plundered.

* * *

Connor walked across the expansive marble lobby and strolled into the bar facing the harbor. He had showered and changed at Alex's place after the miserable fishing expedition. He now just wanted a drink and a quiet place to think. A dark, empty corner would work just fine.

Alex had informed him of some exciting developments, and now they had to plan the next steps, which would not be easy, considering the typical government interference in situations like this one. The one thing he was quite sure of was that he didn't place any faith in the Bahamian government's fairness or process of confidentiality.

He pulled a notebook from his briefcase and began to make plans for the next few days. He tried to keep his mind busy, but again, as always, the sorrow began to creep in. It was in late-night bars that it tended to happen, when the day was winding down. That's when he thought of her and how much he missed her. They had sat in this very bar together. He shockingly realized that probably on this very sofa he had held her. She had traveled with him frequently in the past as he visited clients. The Bahamas had been a favored destination for both of them. He tried to force the thought away and concentrate on his work.

She had died on 9/11. He still had the message on his phone. He played it from time to time.

Connor ran an emerging-market trading desk for a large investment bank and was based in New York City. Although he oversaw many traders and salesmen, his main job was building solid relationships with clients, so he traveled a great deal. Many of these clients were based in the Caribbean, where he had focused his career for the last twenty years. On September 11, 2001, he was in Jamaica. He had returned to his hotel later that evening after a fishing trip with a group of bankers, oblivious to the carnage being perpetrated in New York. He had immediately tried to call her, but there was no answer. Then he saw a message on his mobile phone.

"Connor, something's happening! There is smoke all over the place. I'm scared but I love you so much!"

He never saw his wife or spoke to her again. Much later, he spoke to the police about what had happened to her. It seems most of the people on that floor were unable to get down the stairs blocked by wreckage. She probably jumped, as the fire was intense. He shivered again. The emotional pain was still raw.

He realized again that a tear was rolling down his face. "It's been a long time," he said aloud. "You need to move on with your life. She's gone," he added.

Signaling to the waiter, he downed his drink and ordered another. *It's going to be another long night.* There were several women across the bar who kept stealing glances his way, but he wasn't interested, had not been in a long time. Work was his only pleasure these days, but it was starting to get old.

The second drink helped, and he realized he could not get much done late in the evening. He would need his strength for the following day's activities, so he folded his notebook and picked up the letter from his great-aunt he had received from an attorney in Nassau a month ago. He remembered her face only vaguely, as he had not seen her for probably forty years. She had died when he was a child. Even then he mainly remembered her special cakes with the icing on them that he loved so much, and the large kitchen with such wonderfully strange utensils in that old Victorian house. He had been quite shocked when the attorney for the trust had called.

"Your aunt Clara selected you as trustee for an offshore trust before she died. She didn't want this letter delivered until you were forty-five, and it's yours now. Please come to Nassau and let me hand-deliver it to you as she requested."

"Dear Connor," the letter read, "I want to tell you about your relationship to Aaron Burr."

CHAPTER THREE

May 15, 1698
St. Mary's Island, Madagascar

Captain Kidd stood on the deck of the *Adventure Galley*. The hot African sun warmed his leathered, tanned face, and he braced himself against the ship's railing. He had been drinking rum and was angry.

The voyage had been a very unlucky one. There was no booty to speak of. Two years of chasing pirates around the world and really not much to show for it.

"I knew we sailed from England under an unlucky star," Kidd muttered to himself.

His nemesis, the pirate Captain Robert Culliford, had eluded him for months around the Indian Ocean. Kidd harbored an old grudge against Culliford, who had stolen his ship while he was ashore in Antigua years before. Now, in a twist of fate, Kidd had by chance found Culliford's ship moored off St. Mary's Island weeks earlier.

The *Adventure Galley*, however, had recently captured a Moorish vessel, the *Quedeh Merchant*. It was commanded by the French, so it was technically legal. However, the owner was not French and was making big waves about the theft of his ship and cargo. He was a powerful Arab businessman. Kidd didn't know it, but his luck was turning from bad to worse.

The *Quedeh Merchant* was a huge vessel and was loaded with expensive fabrics and other goods. The East India Tea Company was being pressured severely to return it. The booty was tainted. Kidd had no chance to know he was being branded a pirate not only in London but throughout the world. His benefactors had betrayed him to save their own skins and disowned knowledge of his mission.

Kidd in no way could return the ship and prize money now. It was too late. The crew would not allow it. They had waited too long.

Too long indeed.

Opposite him were one hundred of his men. He had just ordered them to attack Culliford now that Kidd's other prize ships had made the harbor of St. Mary's Island off the Madagascar coast and he had more men and firepower. Kidd hoped to claim a real pirate prize once and for all.

Culliford, however, had been holed up on St. Mary's with him for months and was no fool. He had been working Kidd's crew through surrogates when they went ashore to enjoy the pleasurable native company.

The island was a pirate paradise. Beautiful beaches flanked by palm trees and exotic wildlife made it an idyllic scene. In addition, the natives were very friendly. A man could take a temporary wife for as little as a silk shawl or a nail. The island was square in the middle of the East India shipping lanes and had a natural protected harbor, and they had plenty of rum.

Most of the crew refused Kidd's order and decided to turn pirate and join Culliford. During his entire voyage, Kidd had used the force of his personality to keep the crew in line and to keep them honest. This time he could not do it. They had been two years without pay. They wanted off Kidd's pirate-hunting mission and on to Culliford's hedonistic voyage wherever they might end up. Most pirates chose the short, exciting life of a buccaneer over the long toils of an honest day's work.

"We would rather fire ten guns into you!" they shouted at Kidd.

His dream of returning to London in glory and with treasure was dashed.

"We have had a parley, and we've decided to align ourselves with Captain Culliford. You, my dear Captain Kidd, are hereby ordered to leave the ship with your loyal crew and go ashore. You should consider yourself lucky to leave with your life!" announced his old first mate.

The mutineers left his ship to join Culliford's band of thieves, and reveled in the rum and sex on shore. Many of them married several temporary wives and lost themselves on the beach in debauchery. Worst of all, they looted all of Kidd's ships, taking weapons, rigging, food, water, and anything else of value. They loaded the loot onto the *Mocha Frigate* and sailed away with Captain Culliford.

Kidd was left with the Moorish prize ship, the four-hundred-ton *Quedeh Merchant*, and a twenty-man loyal crew to sail back to London with the little treasure he had left. He poached whatever rigging and sails he could from the *Adventure Galley* and constructed more sails from sackcloth taken from the cargo. His sails became a multicolored rigging made of quilts. The *Adventure Galley* was ordered burned, as she had become riddled with worms.

If attacked, he had enough men to man only two or three of the thirty-plus guns. He renamed his new ship the *Adventure Prize*.

* * *

June 11, 2018

The acrid black smoke billowed through the office doorway like an angel of death, covering everything on the 101st floor in its path. In seconds he could not see his hand in front of him, and fell to the floor to try to continue breathing. He could hear his colleagues shrieking and begging for help, but he could not offer any. The red-hot air burned his lungs as they ingested the poisonous fumes. The outside windows shattered, sending thousands of deadly shards of glass raining down around him. *I'm going to die*, he thought. The building's foundation began to shudder violently; he could feel the tower swaying. He drowned in horror as he felt the floor disappear below his feet. He screamed.

Connor awoke sweating and holding tightly to the sheet matted into a ball. He was drenched and had been screaming again. He could almost still hear the screams echoing off the walls. He looked around the room in the blackness.

What hotel am I in now? he asked himself. In the pitch blackness, his eyes adjusted, and he could make out the desk across the hotel room. Slowly his memory returned, and he was aware of his surroundings.

Ah, Bahamas. I'm in Nassau.

He sat up in the bed and swung his feet over the side, and reached for the water on the nightstand to quench his thirst. He had drunk too much again. Clumsily, Connor made his way to the bathroom to relieve himself.

The nightmares had been almost every night in the beginning but now had begun to lessen somewhat. His therapist had helped with that. God, how he missed Emily, even though it had been over ten years since her death. "I'm so sorry you had to go through that, babe," he muttered out loud to no one.

He tried to focus. He tried to think of the business at hand.

Aunt Clara informed him through the letter written forty years ago that he was descended from Aaron Burr through her side of the family. Connor smiled at himself as he thought of the twinkle in her eye and the obvious secrets she had kept her entire life. She had been the trustee of an offshore entity that he found out included a good deal of money and other documents safeguarded in the Bahamas.

The most interesting of them all, however, was Burr's personal journal. Clara had selected Connor from all of her other family members to be the one to continue on as trustee upon his forty-fifth birthday. *She always did take a special interest in me*, he thought.

Connor took a flight to the Bahamas the day after the attorney had called, and he arrived via taxi at the prominent law firm in downtown Nassau. It was an unusually cloudy day, as the next tropical storm was passing south of the islands on its way to extinction in Mexico. He was disappointed. He had expected tropical bliss.

The overweight tourists off the cruise ships were massing in front of the shops on Bay Street, clogging the thoroughfare for the locals. They were buying T-shirts, rum, and various trinkets.

I guess it pays the bills, he decided.

He was led into an ornately decorated boardroom with ancient dark wooden pilasters lining the walls. There was a long boardroom table with coffee and tea laid out pleasantly. Elegantly bound books adorned the bookshelves.

An older Englishman arrived seconds later and introduced himself. He then formally passed the trustee duties on to Connor and put himself at Connor's service. "Our fees are taken care of by the trust," he said matter-of-factly. He then laid an old ornate wooden box in front of Connor, opened the ancient padlock with a shiny brass key, and left the room.

Connor opened it.

The journal was fascinating; Connor was not sure of the last time it had been held. *Did Clara ever read it?* If so, she'd never let on.

The manuscript told of Burr's time as vice president, the duel with Hamilton, and most important, the time he spent out west trying to start another country. Connor read for more than four hours that day. He then spent another two days speaking with the attorneys and understanding his duties as trustee. That was a month ago.

Connor climbed back into bed and shut his eyes. As usual,

however, the alcohol from the night before would keep him awake. His head was throbbing like a jackhammer. It would be another long night.

* * *

March 2, 1699
Atlantic Ocean

Kidd awoke before sunrise; actually he really never went to sleep. He lay in his berth on the nearly deserted ship, listening as always to the sounds the vessel made. These sounds told him many things. The health of the ship, the mood of his crew, and the temper of the sea were all told to him in a brief instant by listening. He rose in the blackness of his cabin.

The days had passed one after the other and now ran together in a haze of time. He had taken on more crew members at Annobón, in the Gulf of Guinea, but still was dreadfully short of men to run the huge ship. It was a miracle they had gotten this far. They were nearing the Caribbean Sea.

The ocean was fairly calm, but there was a west wind blowing. The *Adventure Prize* was making about five knots. The crew, or rather what was left of his crew, was exhausted. They had been making their way for almost four months now across the Atlantic from St. Mary's Island, only twenty-plus men and boys to sail this monster of a ship. It was an almost impossible task, but Captain Kidd had always asked the impossible. One man had died of exhaustion. They were getting almost no sleep, rotating ten men every six hours. Only the will to survive kept them going. Their dreams of riches and booty had long been dashed.

This morning, however, Kidd felt something. Something was going to happen today. Something good was going to happen. He made his way to the deck.

The sun was breaking over the horizon as he approached the

perch of the night watchman scanning the ocean with a spyglass. "Good mornin to ya," said Kidd. The exhausted man could barely mumble something in return. Official manners had gone out the window, yet the crew had bonded and worked together as well as possible.

Kidd fumbled in his pockets for his pipe and tobacco. He would start the day with a smoke.

"Sail!" shouted the watchman.

Kidd jerked his head around to where the man was pointing, and saw several white specks in the distance. "Raise whatever sails we have left," he shouted. "We'll try and run from them."

Naval engagements during the seventeenth century typically moved in slow motion until the bitter end. Ships targeted by pirates or opposing navies could try to outrun their antagonist for days, depending on the wind. This tactic was used if they felt their enemy had superior firepower. Once the target was within range, however, the endgame was quick and violent. The loser was either sunk or boarded and taken as a prize. The fate of the crew rested with the captain of the victorious ship.

Kidd didn't have the crew to engage one ship much less several. His only hope was to outrun them. *Perhaps I will never see Sarah and my daughter again.*

"There are three ships, and they're not moving, Captain," responded his first mate. "They're in trouble. The sails are not being tended to. I see no one on board."

This changed the situation altogether.

Kidd stared at the vessels lying dormant on the horizon; his greed got the best of him. He had to make a decision.

"We will board them," he said with determination.

CHAPTER FOUR

March 25, 1699
West Indies

Kidd didn't dare try to off-load the ship in the daylight. The night was his friend. He didn't trust strangers to help him either. He had anchored in the evening two weeks earlier on the eastern unpopulated side of the island, and to his knowledge had not been discovered. There was not a large population on this side of the archipelago.

The ship, however, stood out in the twilight even with her sails furled, like a series of crosses highlighting the horizon. The small landmass of the island seemed misplaced in the vast ocean surrounding it. The sun was setting now in the west. The dark green of the lush vegetation created a stark contrast to the deep blue sea surrounding the land.

Luckily, for this task, it was positive he had such a skeleton crew. More than ninety men had left his legitimate privateering mission to turn pirate, and they had missed the biggest score of all. Although it was almost impossible to sail his four-hundred-ton ship the *Adventure Prize* with a crew of twenty-plus, he had done it. He had done it through sheer force of will.

Captain Kidd was an extremely resourceful man.

What the pirate Culliford, or anyone else for that matter, would never know was that Kidd had secured three prizes during the trip back from Africa to the Caribbean. He and his crew found them roped together floating aimlessly in the Atlantic, three Spanish galleons on a return trip from the Spanish Main.

Upon boarding they found all of the crew dead. They had been dead for some time, according to the decomposition of the bodies. There was nothing alive on the vessels. Even the rats had died of starvation. Kidd knew what had killed the crew. In addition to starvation and dehydration, it was the plague. Most of the victims had evidence of a gushing of blood from the nose, a clear indication of the Black Death.

Kidd had a decision to make. Did he take a chance on infecting his crew by searching the ships? Or did he just leave and burn the floating morgues? He chose the former. He ordered his crew to search the ships quickly.

The shocking find was that each of the holds was filled with gold bullion. Obviously the gold had been mined and shaped in Latin America, and the bars were being shipped back to the homeland to fill the King's coffers. The Spanish were very efficient at harvesting for the Crown the precious metal from their colonies. There was no mint in the New World, so the treasure was shipped home in the form of bullion. Trillions of today's dollars' worth of gold and silver were ferried back to Spain over the span of a century. The Spanish in turn used the immense wealth to expand their empire and launch wars across the globe.

Kidd could now repay his investors a thousand times over. He was elated. The crew was overjoyed. In their exhausted, delirious state, they reveled in thoughts of the luxurious future to come.

The *Adventure Prize* was a huge ship and almost empty, so he had the gold transferred aboard her. There was gold everywhere—in the hold, on the deck, everywhere.

Now that he had reached his destination, he would return home in another ship that he could purchase somewhere inconspicuously so as not to invite questions regarding the Moorish galleon. He was immensely rich. He still clung to the notion that he could save his three-year mission, make money for his backers, and return home a hero. He longed to hold Sarah and his daughter.

Kidd was no stranger to this place. He had been depositing gold, silver, and precious stones here on the island for almost twenty years during his frequent travels around the world and multiple years at sea. Many moons ago, he had defended the island from the French. He had plundered their ships unlucky enough to sail nearby. At that time, the governor of the island had even given Kidd his own ship, the *Blessed William*, only to have Culliford steal it a few years later.

Yes, he had deposited much wealth here. It was his insurance policy, his nest egg. He wondered if he would ever get to enjoy it. This trip was the largest deposit ever, immense. The Spanish galleons he had captured saw to that. This would be the last of many nights needed to bring the treasure to shore.

The longboat was heavily laden and sat deep in the water as they set out from the ship. There was no natural harbor here. The waves attacked the craft mercilessly, soaking the sailors with the salty water. Tonight, the current was worse than on their previous trips, and they were tired.

Through brute strength the men persevered and eventually approached the shore. Kidd ordered a brief rest.

William Kidd and two of his most trusted men and several slaves strolled onto the beach. Their sea legs betrayed them, and it took a few minutes to get used to the change in circumstances.

When he had arrived weeks earlier, he approached his usual contact on the island to provide the necessary men and materials. He learned that his old friend had died a year earlier; however, his son was eager to help, for a price of course. Since then, the son was there on time every evening and provided the number of mules requested for this now routine exercise, twenty to be exact. He hoped they would be enough for this last load.

They spent the better part of two hours hauling the precious metal from the boat to the mule train. Then the trek up the side of the mountain began.

It was actually not a mountain. The natural edifice they were climbing was the caldera of a long-dormant volcano. The vegetation was dense, like in a jungle, and the first night they had to cut their way through. It was difficult if not almost impossible work. They had made this trip every night for two weeks now, so the path was becoming well worn.

It's been so long since I have been here, he reminisced to himself the first night out. What has it been? Three years?

They reached their destination right before sunrise and began the reverse procedure of off-loading the metal into the cave. It took almost three hours this time to finish the process. They were exhausted. Kidd surveyed the cave, remembering and checking on his past deposits. Nothing had been disturbed. When finished, he took one last satisfied look at the treasure and made his way back to the opening.

Now it was time for the dirty work. He could not afford the chance that anyone would know where the gold was stored.

He ordered the slaves to the back of the natural cave. The two white men with him pulled out their multiple muskets they had previously loaded. He saw the eyes of the poor, wretched men widen. His men began firing. Only three white souls left the cave alive. They left the bodies where they fell, a natural deterrent to the superstitious natives if the gold was found. *It will be harder to man my leaking ship without the additional help, but it is a risk I have to take*, he thought.

They made the trek back to the shore quickly and rowed

themselves to the ship. No questions were asked by the crew. No one said a word. They knew better.

Captain Kidd then ordered the mainsails unfurled, and the ship quietly moved away from Nevis.

* * *

> Historically, money in the form of currency has predominated. Usually (gold or silver) coins of intrinsic value commensurate with the monetary unit (<u>commodity money</u>) have been the norm. By contrast, modern currency, as <u>fiat money</u>, is intrinsically worthless.
>
> —Wikipedia

* * *

June 21, 2018
New York City

Connor stepped off the Metro-North commuter train with the hordes jockeying for position. Unfortunately, the train passengers had disembarked on the lower level. This meant that he had to fight the throng of people to climb the stairs to the upper level of Grand Central Terminal. The time was 6:32 a.m.; the train was right on time. *At least that still works*, he noted as he slowly put one foot in front of the other up the metal steps, all the while feeling like he was in a herd of cattle. There was a slow, elderly person in front of him, and that only added to his frustration.

What New York does to you, he thought as he exited the stairwell. Grand Central was as loud as ever this morning. He almost collided with several other commuters as he crossed the main floor and started up the stairs to the western entrance.

He arrived at the trading floor twenty minutes later, having made the hike across Midtown Manhattan. Strangely enough, the walk always unnerved him, as he pictured himself incinerated by the latest terrorist attack on the city. There was something vulnerable about being a pedestrian in the city.

It will be nuclear at some point, he concluded. It's inevitable.

But the biggest threat to the U.S. at this point was not a nuclear weapon, although probable down the road; it was the economy and the debt situation.

Over the last several years, the debt had exploded. The initial estimates at the beginning of the decade were for a trillion a year for ten years, and then the deficit was to be reduced. This was not the case. It was 2018, and the total outstanding debt for the United States was over $20 trillion. The health care bill and other entitlements had cost much more than the Congressional Budget Office had predicted. No one could fathom this amount.

The uncertainty this yoke created restrained growth in the economy, which reduced economic growth and tax revenues. It created a vicious downward spiral.

It was a nightmare, and no politician seemed to be able to step up and lead the country out of the morass.

For centuries nation-states had based their currencies on something of value. Typically this store of value was a precious metal, usually gold, silver, or copper. This was no longer the case. No developed country in the world used this system. It was all fiat money, the supply of which was created by a central bank or monetary authority. They could print all the money they wanted.

The problem with printing money was that if too much was printed, the currency became worthless. There are examples throughout history of this happening, in the German Weimar Republic for instance.

With the surrender of Germany following World War I, the Weimar Republic began printing money at an alarming rate to pay its war reparations under the Treaty of Versailles. At the end of the war, the German mark was exchanged at 4.2 per U.S. dollar. At the end of 1923, the rate was 1 million marks per U.S. dollar. Hundreds of factories were employed just to print the paper money needed to keep up with demand.

Obviously unsustainable, the currency was reset to the 4.2 exchange rate in late 1923, but the damage already had been done to the economy. This gave Hitler an opening.

The United States was heading down this path.

This impacted Connor through the bond market.

* * *

> The U.S. government has a technology, called
> a printing press (or today, its electronic equivalent),
> that allows it to produce as many U.S. dollars as it
> wishes at no cost.
> —Ben Bernanke, chairman of the Board of
> Governors of the Federal Reserve System

* * *

Connor ran a group of bond traders and salesmen, who created revenue by trading fixed-income sovereign and corporate securities.

As more debt was created by an issuer and the risk for investors increased, the buyers of this debt required more compensation to take on the risk of being paid back by the creditor—in this case the United States. This caused interest rates to rise, which limited economic growth and reduced the country's standard of living. If not controlled, it became an unsustainable situation.

He put all of this out of his mind as he reached his Bloomberg terminal and began the process of booting up the system. Although he was the boss, he preferred to work out on the floor with his troops rather than holed up in his office. He liked to feel the vibration, the action of the trading floor.

The phones already were ringing off the hook. Overnight the White House had raised the budget deficit estimates for the next year, and the Treasury bond market had tanked. There used to be a strong bid or demand for U.S. Treasuries, due to a flight-to-quality knee-jerk reaction from the market. An investment in U.S. government securities had historically been considered a "risk-free" investment. No more. Now there was panic that rates were going to have to go much higher to attract buyers to fund all of the new debt.

"God, I feel like I'm living under Jimmy Carter," he said sarcastically to himself. He was having trouble getting motivated this morning. The business was slowly becoming not fun anymore.

Connor had returned to New York to take care of the trading desk, but his mind was still in the Bahamas.

He was ripped away from the islands back to New York when the news hit the tape. CNBC announced it first, and the trading floor went crazy.

"Euro currency to dissolve due to sovereign debt crisis," the talking heads grimly proclaimed.

* * *

June 8, 1702
Nevis

Although Nevis was a mostly dormant volcano, there had been some activity ten years prior. There were also numerous hot springs and fumaroles sprinkled about the island, evidence that geologic activity was still going on deep below.

In addition, over one hundred years of intense deforestation to support the immensely profitable sugar industry on the island had made the soil on the dormant caldera quite unstable. The coral reefs protecting the shoreline were beginning to break apart as they died from lack of runoff from the now gone vegetation, leaving less and less protection for the coastline from the savage sea.

It was a little-known fact that at this time, the West Indies sugar and slave trade provided more income to the English Crown than trade from all of the North American colonies combined. The cane in Nevis was particularly valued, as it had a higher level of sugar content than that in neighboring islands. This produced a bountiful crop to provide the ladies and gentlemen in England sugar cubes for their coffee.

Nevis was also a base of operations for the English privateers and pirates preying on French and Spanish ships in the region. Soon the French would invade the island to put a stop to this and change the sugar trade forever.

Whether it was a volcanic event or a mudslide caused by the unstable mountainside, we will never know. A thundering boom followed by the crashing sound of trees snapping emanated from the mountainside. A dark mass could be seen shifting down the eastern side of the caldera. The mudslide covered all entry points to Captain Kidd's cave.

CHAPTER FIVE

New York City

Connor relaxed into the wonderfully padded chair at his favorite watering hole in the city, The Campbell Apartment. His body melted into the soft covering as the day's stress poured out of him. He had selected his usual spot in the dark, southwestern corner of the cavernous space; it was after ten o'clock in the evening, and he had put in a long day. The cute waitress brought him a drink. He loved the tight-fitting, black, slim dresses they wore. The contours of her body were easily seen and imagined. As she bent over and delivered his cocktail, something stirred inside him. *It's been too long*, he thought.

Emily came back into his mind. He pushed her away.

I'm not going there tonight.

The bar used to be the personal salon of one wealthy New Yorker named John Campbell. He had leased the space from Cornelius Vanderbilt inside of Grand Central Terminal. It was not an apartment per se, but he entertained guests there after spending a fortune to design and renovate the place in the early twentieth century. Hand-painted plaster ceilings, leaded windows, mahogany woodwork, and Persian rugs dominated the thirty-five-hundred-square-foot open area.

I'm always shocked by the magnificence of this place, Connor reflected. It was very crowded, and he was glad his assistant had called and reserved a table. He frequently entertained clients here.

But tonight he was not enjoying it. He was simply tired. His thoughts drifted back to his recent time in the Bahamas.

Connor had spent several days going over his findings from the journal and other effects from the trust. The most shocking revelation was that Burr had stumbled on something of great value.

In the chest, Connor had found a leather pouch that was covered with a dark stain. "Who knows what this pouch has been through," he said to himself. He carefully laid it aside.

Also inside were several very old and delicate parchments. He unfolded them slowly and felt guilty handling something that should have been in the Smithsonian. *Maybe in time they will be.* He laid them out on the table unfolded.

He realized immediately that the parchments were maps that led to multiple locations around the Caribbean. "Treasure maps? You have to be kidding me!" he exclaimed aloud.

The first was obviously pointing to a location in the Bahamas, near one of the out islands.

"I need to bring Alex into this."

Connor had the trust company staff make a photocopy of the first map and then replaced everything in the chest. For security reasons and to be safe, he would tell Alex only about the first map and nothing about where it came from.

I wonder what is there, he thought as he exited the law firm's front entrance and walked in the hot sun down Bay Street back to the Hilton. He thought of the many pirates who came to Nassau hundreds of years ago to trade and barter the goods they had seized from other ships.

Connor was brought back into the present at the bar as his cell phone, which he had set on the small table, began to vibrate and work its way toward the edge. He watched it for a moment. He

33

feared being called back to work, and hesitated. Then he noticed the number was from the Bahamas, and he grabbed it before it fell off the table, and answered.

It was Alex.

"You need to come back down immediately," he somewhat demanded. "I think I've found it."

Alex had a long history in the Bahamas, although he was Russian. His hobby outside of trading was treasure hunting throughout the Caribbean. He had many finds to his credit, although nothing yet of any significant value. However, hunting for sunken treasure was his passion, as well as restoring old boats.

After leaving the law firm, Connor had shown Alex the map and asked if he could help. The map was obviously very old and the cartography was primitive. There were hundreds of small cays in the Bahamas, and it would be difficult to find this exact spot. That's what they had discussed on the tower of his boat coming back from the fishing trip. Alex didn't have an answer then, but now he thought he might.

"I'll be down on the first flight in the morning," said Connor.

He hung up the phone and quickly finished his drink. He was excited for a brief moment.

Then his exhaustion got the better of him. He had to calm his nerves and decompress from the long, intense New York day. The alcohol would do that for him. He ordered another and undressed the waitress with his eyes.

* * *

January 11, 1765
Nevis

The small boy followed his friend up the vine-covered incline. She was a slave child from the village near the mountain, so was more adept than he at scaling the steep hill. She was fast. He tried

34

to keep up. The vegetation was thick, and he was having a hard time making his way through it.

As he looked up after her, he could see the top of the thirty-two-hundred-foot volcano covered in a cloudy mist. Negotiating the thin path was difficult, and he was tired.

"Alexander, we are almost there!" she shouted in her thick, native Caribbean accent. Monkeys unused to intruders barked at the pair as they struggled higher through the vegetation. They were angry these humans were trespassing on their territory, and were making the most god-awful racket. They flew back and forth across the overhead branches in a rattled state. *There are hundreds of them*, the boy agonized. It was scary.

As he looked back, he could see the smoke from the many sugar mills rising up from the lush, green coastal floor at the base of the old volcano. Several ships were anchored off Charlestown, the main civilized area on the island. St. Kitts beckoned a short distance away across the sea, another island named after Christopher Columbus.

He was breathing hard now and sweating profusely. He was a slight, thin child with reddish hair, of Scottish descent. Most people considered him delicate.

The girl had come to him while he was walking home from his Jewish tutor's house. The illegitimate boy's parents had decided long ago to have him tutored instead of attending school on the island, where he was born. Taking off for the afternoon up into the mountains with a slave girl was not something that anyone would notice. He had plenty of free time.

"I have a secret place," she taunted him. "Do you want to see?"

They were both approximately ten years old, so the taunt was completely innocent.

"Sure," he had said, and off they went up the mountain.

Nevis was the caldera of a long-smoldering volcano rising out of the Caribbean Sea in the West Indies. Up to this point, the mountain itself had not been thoroughly explored. There were hundreds of caves and natural fissures in the side of the mountain from the fumaroles that opened from time to time. The jungle vegetation covered the entire area thoroughly from the sea to the rim. The two children were about halfway up the side of the volcano and climbing higher. The young boy felt as if he were climbing to the clouds, and in a way he was.

Her wind was better than his, and he was about to turn back when she exclaimed, "We're here!" Her face lit up as she pointed to an opening obscured by the trunks of several huge trees. A few days ago, the hole had been spewing gases from deep below, but the gases had recently stopped and the surrounding rock had cooled.

They slid between the tree trunks and looked into the small cave. The angle of the opening was forty-five degrees downward, and at the right time of day, the sun shone deeply into the hole, providing natural light. The outlines of an underground cavern could be seen.

"Let's go," said the girl as she squeezed in and slid down into the larger opening. The boy followed.

It took some time before their eyes adjusted to the reduced light.

The girl screamed.

Someone had been here before, a long time ago. Someone had died here a long time ago. There were many skeletons with remnants of hair and clothes scattered across the middle of the underground room. Shrunken skin still clung to the bones, making for a ghastly scene.

The girl started shaking and screaming again, speaking erratically about the dead spirits and evil. She scampered out of the cave into the daylight.

The boy remained.

There was something else. He could make out shapes to the rear of the space. He overcame his fear and gingerly stepped over the bodies and walked deeper into the cave in the darkening light. He was curious.

There were many chests stacked in rows. He opened one and caught his breath in shock.

The chests were filled with gold bars.

* * *

Nassau, Bahamas
June 21, 2018

The Nassau night sky was clear as Alex drove up the small alley road that led to the water tower elevated on a hill in the center of town. It was a nice night, but there was not a breeze in sight; the humidity hung like a wool blanket under the full summer moon. The streets were calm tonight but as usual littered with garbage. The drive to the tower did not make a good impression. He was away from the main tourist area, and it showed.

The plants on the side of the road stretched their limbs above the pavement. He could hear music and loud voices coming from the nearby residential area. The lights of the houses brightened with a yellowed electricity.

The water tower was somewhat of an attraction. Visitors routinely climbed the masonry stairs of the stone structure to get a better view of the entire city, as it was the highest point on the island. Tonight, however, Alex's destination was different.

Next to the old water tower there was an even older structure, Fort Fincastle. It had been built by Lord Dunmore in 1793 as part of a series of edifices constructed to protect the city. The design was unique, as it was built to resemble an old paddle-wheeled steamer approaching bow on. A rounded west end with multiple rotating gun emplacements sat opposite the pointed bow of the ship. It was fairly small and meant only as a cannon placement to complete the field of fire over Nassau.

Alex had been born in Russia, but no one would know it by speaking with him. His accent was Bahamian through and through, a real Conchy Joe. His parents had immigrated to the Bahamas when he was a teenager after the Soviet Union disintegrated. He had memories of his country of birth and had visited several times. Russian was spoken in his home, so he could revert to that language at a moment's notice.

His task tonight, however, had nothing to do with his upbringing. It had to do with money.

He drove up the winding, thin, one-lane road that led to the fort complex. The plywood market shops that lined the side of the parking lot were empty and boarded up at this hour. The Bahamians never missed a chance to sell their wares to the tourists who came from the constant flow of cruise ships. In the morning, the booths would be filled with pirated DVDs, handmade wooden toys, jewelry, and other crafts.

There was one official-looking vehicle parked by itself near the stone walls of the fort, a dark sedan. Alex parked his own car across from the market booths and in front of the pointed bow of the structure.

He then strolled carefully to the back entrance, which opened into a small walled outdoor area surrounded by cannons, which pointed upward at a low angle. The rusting steel tracks, which allowed the wheels on the rear end of the cannons to swing, were illuminated in the moonlight.

Alex walked past them and turned right into the bowels of the small concrete center. It looked as though it were an old powder magazine hollowed into the cement core. There was a table in the middle of the room with a large black man sitting on the far side of it. Two fierce-looking bodyguards stood behind him. A single one-bulb light dangled from the ceiling and cast a yellow glow over the damp, ancient space. Alex walked in and said nothing. He acknowledged the man's presence.

"You are late. I don't like to be kept waiting," the black man said. Alex didn't respond. "But let's forget about that and get to the matter at hand. I would like to make you a financial proposition."

"I am open to hearing what you have to say, Mr. Prime Minister," Alex replied.

CHAPTER SIX

Eleuthera, Bahamas

Connor closed the door of the cottage and set the deadbolt. He felt especially at home here. He did not know why. Maybe it was the freedom it offered. The island provided total anonymity and control, just like he liked it. But nothing was permanent; he couldn't stay long. He put that reality out of his mind.

A little bit of heaven never hurt anyone, he thought.

He walked to the cheap rental car he had acquired the day before and drove backwards down the shell-lined driveway. The crunch of the crustaceans' former home was comforting to him in some strange way. Geckos darted in and out of the surrounding scrub brush. The beating sun gave its last gasp, and the shadows were beginning to fall. The air was warm.

He bought the cottage several years ago, after the real estate crisis of 2008. People had stopped coming to the Bahamas and especially Eleuthera. Second homes in the islands were just not a priority.

He was a fan of buying things when no one else wanted them, when they were on sale. Real estate in the Bahamas was in this category after 2008. He had paid a very low price for a run-down cottage on the west coast facing the Atlantic. It was a fixer-upper. He even had his own piece of beach in a secluded, uninhabited lagoon—paradise. The downside was that he did not get to come here as often as he liked.

The long island snaked down from New Providence like a piece of confetti, at its widest a few hundred feet. At the north end was Harbor Island and all of the wealth it brought. It was rumored Bill Gates owned a home there. In the middle was Governor's Harbor, a quaint town without all of the pretension of its northern neighbor. This was near where Connor had bought.

He had flown into Governor's Harbor from New York the day after Alex's call. He planned to meet Alex early the following morning for the trip to the possible treasure site. Connor had spent the night at his cottage to make sure the caretaker was doing his job. He arrived in the early afternoon and spent the day doing small repairs around the house. Now he needed something to eat and a drink, to smell the roses a bit.

He drove to the east coast and snaked his way down the winding road for several miles, then took an offshoot up to a rocky cliff overlooking the ocean. Here was located a small outdoor bar and restaurant. It was the only decent place to eat on this part of the island. Several cars were parked on each side of the driveway. A slight wind from the open window of the car warmed his face.

He parked and walked into the restaurant and took a seat at the empty bar. *Good, I like solitude when I eat*, he thought. Most of the customers were down on the beach. It looked like some kind of wedding party. They were laughing and smiling and having a great time, as people should at a wedding.

The bartender smiled at him. "The usual," Connor said. "And a menu." The bartender brought him a single-malt Scotch. The alcohol did its duty. He began to relax. It wasn't often he was able to relax. Such was the life of a bond trader.

The stress was a curse. The business was very lucrative; however, there were downsides. The bond market could move on the tiniest of things. Economics was the basic driver. Leading indicators of economic activity played the major role. Where do people think the economy is going? It's the perception of the future, not necessarily the reality.

Connor noticed everything: how many cars were at the hotel, the size of the crowds at the airport, the price of a beer; all were bits of information. He traveled so much that he had a chance to see these variables in multiple locations. It was his way of making his own decisions on how things were going economically. It was a way to do a real-time check on the experts' opinions.

He was halfway through his meal when he noticed a very attractive woman sitting alone in the screened-in area off the deck. Not just attractive. She was drop-dead gorgeous. She had finished her meal and was now slowly nursing her drink, staring out at the ocean. The sun was near setting, and the whitecaps from the breakers glistened in the evening light as they crashed onto the beach. The sound was soothing.

She was darkly tanned with long, dark, shiny hair, which complemented the simple sundress she was wearing. Her body was slim but shapely. She seemed sad.

Initially Connor ignored her as always, but something made him reconsider. *Maybe it's now or never*, he thought. *Maybe it's time.*

The sun touched the blue horizon. He got up and walked over to her. The bartender saw him leave and raised an eyebrow in surprise.

She turned her head as he approached, and he pointed to the sunset with his drink.

"These should never be watched alone, you know. Hi, I'm Connor."

She smiled and replied, "But what if I want to be alone?"

His smile dropped. "Well then I will go back to my lonely place at the bar," said Connor with not-so-feigned disappointment apparent in his voice.

"Oh, what the hell, sit down," she said. "I'm Katherine. Call me Kate." She waved to the bartender for another drink, and Connor ordered another as well.

Connor took a chair across the table as their drinks arrived. "Thanks, Hal," he quipped. The bartender smiled.

"Good to see you back in the game. Take care of him now; he's a regular," Hal said to Kate, and then walked off with a smile.

"What's that about?" she asked.

"Oh, I've been coming here for years and usually just sit at the bar. I think he's impressed with my opening line. It works every time. Took me years to develop it."

A smile appeared on her face.

"Well this is my first time here. I just drove up from the science institute on the south end. I had to get a little civilization. I've been living in the commune for several weeks."

"Well that's different! So, Kate, what are you researching there?" asked Connor with genuine interest.

"Sunken treasure," she replied.

Connor almost choked on his drink.

"Tell me more," he requested, now sitting up in his chair, having forgotten about the sunset.

"Well as you know these cays are filled with wrecks from the last few hundred years. No one has really made a sincere effort to catalogue them all. I am. In addition, I am working with the scientists at the institute to develop ways to find and salvage these wrecks without destroying the reefs. The government is very interested in this and has given me a grant. I'm here for three months. And then back to Boston."

"How would you like to go on a treasure hunt tomorrow?" he asked.

* * *

It took three hours to reach Brigantine Cays, a group of small islands off Great Exuma, south of Nassau, the capital of New Providence Island. Connor got to know Kate as they cruised down the Atlantic. He found they had a lot in common. He felt something that he hadn't felt in a long time and was smitten by her beauty.

They dropped anchor at noon. The ocean sparkled in the sunlight, and the sun glared.

Earlier in the day, Alex had arrived at Governor's Harbor pier in Eleuthera to pick up Connor at the designated time. Kate was waiting there when Connor arrived ten minutes before the hour. The normal commerce at the small port was thriving early in the morning. The wharf was bustling with activity. Of course, the term "bustling" was relative when speaking of the Bahamas. They received several inquisitive looks from the locals.

"I thought you might not make it," Connor announced to her. "But I'm glad you did!"

And he *was* glad, very happy as a matter of fact. Her long hair glistened in the noonday sun. She was wearing khaki shorts and a loose-fitting cotton top. Her tan skin contrasted with the white fabric beautifully.

"Are you kidding? I wouldn't miss this for the world," she replied, winking at him.

His heart jumped a beat.

Alex was not happy. He made that very clear as Kate went to get her gear from her car.

"You should have cleared it with me first!" he reprimanded. "No one else should be involved with this. You don't know anything about her!"

"Look, Alex, I understand what you are saying, but she could be of help. She knows the area and has expertise in this type of thing. And for God's sake, look at her! Help me out here! You know it's rare I find someone I like."

"I don't like it!" Alex replied. "But I guess I have no choice." He boarded the boat in a foul mood.

Connor and Kate came aboard as well. Alex didn't say much until they reached the cays.

"He doesn't want me here, does he?" she asked Connor on the way down. "I can understand that."

"He's become very paranoid lately," answered Connor. "I'm not sure what is going on—other than just good security precautions. Look, this is how this will work. The find is ours. If you can help in some way today, we will give you a cut. Alex and I will decide what your contribution is worth. Fair enough?"

"That works for me," she said happily. "How long have you and Alex known each other?"

"A long time, ten years," Connor replied. "We've been through hell and back together dealing with crisis after crisis in the markets over the last decade, and have helped each other out from time to time. I trust him completely."

"What's his background?" she asked.

"He was born in Russia, and his parents moved here after the Soviet Union collapsed. He's become quite the Bahamian citizen, a real promoter of the islands, if you will. He works hard on his island persona. Close friends are hard to find in this world."

"Yes they are," she said wistfully. Connor wondered what the background behind her tone was and if she had lost something as well in her past, but he didn't intrude on her thoughts.

They arrived in the Brigantine Cays three hours later and were able to anchor in waist-deep water near the small cay. Connor was always amazed at the piercing blue, shallow water surrounding each of the Bahamian islands. They hopped over the side of the boat and waded through the warm ocean to the shore. Silvery fish darted in and out around them as they made their way to the dry land.

The cay was a small island about the length of a football field and shaped like an oarlock with two parallel prongs jutting out into the sea. The sandy soil covered calcium carbonate rock, which poked out of the soil in spots where the two fingers of the island met in the middle. The Bahamas were formed from coral reefs that became dry land when the sea level dropped thousands of years ago.

The three of them walked to the center of the cay, where the rock formations were the largest. Iguanas roamed free and paused to study the strange beings invading their home but did not seem disturbed. They had not learned to fear humans.

Alex had used the drawing Connor provided from the trust to match an aerial overlay of the Bahamas. This island fit the map perfectly.

The ground was full of sharp edges, as the elements had carved their own designs into the rock over the centuries. Connor felt them cut into the rubber soles of his shoes as they explored the island.

"The tide will be high in twenty minutes," said Alex. "That should give us several hours before we have to get back to the boat. I don't want the boat to be beached out here."

"Agreed," replied Connor. "Although, the high tide may cover some of the search area."

The back side of the cay facing away from the parallel jetties backed right into the ocean. The water had created a series of caves above and below the waterline.

"Why don't we spread out?" suggested Alex. "This will take some time to search."

They searched for two hours every nook and cranny of the rock formation, which was difficult, as much of it was underwater. The tide began to draw out.

"Maybe it's a wild goose chase," said Connor as he and Alex stood on top of the rocks and looked out over the ocean. The beaming sun was taking its toll.

"Maybe so," said Alex. "Where's Kate?" he added.

Kate was deep inside one of the small caves; her neck hurt from bending over and avoiding the pain of banging her head into the sharp rocks above her. She had found nothing again. She began making her way out.

As she stepped out of the cave and across an opening to the sea below, she glanced down into the shallow water lapping into the base of the rock. The retreating tide had reduced the water in the pocket underneath her. A curious shape caught her eye. It was a thin rock that was almost too rounded. She had seen formations like this on many of her other successful expeditions, and crawled down to the water.

She reached down into the water and grabbed the rock; it was encrusted with minerals that had been deposited over the decades.

I was right, she thought. *It's a coin.* She slipped it into her pocket.

She moved to climb back up the rock through the opening when she saw that underneath the rock above there was another cave she had not noticed, extending back under the upper formation. It was fairly large but had a small opening; the chamber was flooded during the tides, but the water was starting to drain out. She looked inside and saw the remains of an iron and wooden chest.

She crawled into the space and pulled her flashlight out to search the area underneath the pieces of metal and iron hinges. There was nothing there. Whatever was left of the chest was empty.

Upon leaving the cave, she noticed a small, square shape near the rim on the ledge leading to the water. She put the metal object in her pocket and climbed out of the cave.

"It's been moved," she said as she climbed on top of the rock formation and approached Connor and Alex.

She pulled the coin and the metal object from her pocket. Alex's eyes grew wide.

"Show us where you found it!" he demanded.

They searched the entire area again but found nothing more; no clues either as to when or who had taken the treasure.

"It's an American quarter eagle," informed Kate as she cleaned the coin in a small vat of chemicals she had brought in her gear. "Probably eighteenth century."

She handed the coin to Alex as he drove the boat back to Nassau. The sea was calm today.

He turned it over in his hands. "You are correct," he reluctantly muttered. "And I must give you credit; I underestimated you."

"You had every right to be concerned about me," she replied. "The coin is yours and Connor's."

"I want to find the real treasure," he added.

"Then perhaps this will help." She pulled, also from the vat of solvents, a small, silver container the size of a matchbox and handed it to Alex. He looked it over and handed it to Connor. There were initials engraved in the top.

"It's a snuff pouch, maybe late seventeenth century—more like eighteenth," commented Kate. "I found it in the cave as well."

"AB," said Alex. "Aaron Burr."

"Yes, now we know he was there," said Connor. "But where is the treasure?"

Connor then looked at Alex with sincere doubt and concern on his face. Alex saw the expression.

Connor had never told Alex about his connection to Aaron Burr.

The boat continued on the path back to Eleuthera. Not much was said on the trip home; everyone was tired. The sun had taken its toll on them. Connor and Kate did not notice the large, white yacht that had been off the coast of the Brigantine Cays turn and begin to follow them. Alex stole an occasional glance at the craft but did not say anything.

* * *

February 28, 1700
New York

Lord Bellomont was in pain as he sat in his favorite chair in front of the fireplace. The flames crackled, but the warmth only exacerbated his illness. He pulled his foot away from the heat, hoping that it would help. It didn't. His big toe felt like it had a knife stuck in the joint. The pain radiated up his leg. He didn't know it, but he had only a few days remaining on this earth. The hour was late in more ways than one.

He had woken up at 3:00 a.m. and tossed and turned for a while before deciding to head downstairs to the fire. His wife had grown used to his nightly stirrings, so she slept soundly. He could hear shouting from the pub located around the corner from his home in the city. He longed for the days when he was healthy enough for a drink.

He was a successful, well-fed man living a life of luxury. All of the red meat and wine had led to the gout. The pain was unbearable, and he could no longer sleep more than a few hours. Being the governor of three territories in the New World had taken a toll on his health. New York was so cold this time of year.

At least I have Kidd rotting in the town jail. The thought brought him some smug satisfaction.

Captain Kidd had become a thorn in his side, and the situation would need careful attention to achieve the desired outcome.

Bellomont was one of the original backers of the mission and wanted to receive his share of the booty. However, Kidd had become a pariah internationally. He was labeled a pirate. The British East India Company despised him, and Bellomont could not afford to be tarred with Kidd's reputation. Well, maybe he could have his cake and eat it too. He could find the treasure himself and then throw Kidd to the wolves and make his masters happy.

He had uncovered several buried chests with a sizable amount of treasure on Gardiner's Island and elsewhere since Kidd had turned himself in. Kidd had buried these upon his return to New England and willingly gave Bellomont the location. The mother lode, however, was yet to be found. Bellomont had sent a ship to Antigua to find the *Quedeh Merchant*, but the captain had come back with only a burnt rope from where the ship had been tied. The ship had been torched and burned to the keel.

Bellomont was not a happy man. And the gout really hurt.

I will send him to London to be hanged, he decided in a fit of psychotic rage.

CHAPTER SEVEN

March 31, 1780
Nevis

The small boats came at night one by one from the ships anchored offshore. They slaved their way across the breakers crashing in front of them and then disgorged their men onto the beach and waited. Many of the men were slaves.

The caravans went up the mountain after sunset and were down before daybreak. There were twenty African men in each, led by five white officers. It was backbreaking work. It was also a very well-planned operation and executed precisely. The boats were loaded onshore, and their precious cargo quietly ferried to the waiting vessels.

The ships, once filled with gold, slipped out of the protection of the reefs around Nevis and proceeded to their destinations. The slaves worked as crew. The officers were trusted friends and professionals. The gold was being moved for a reason.

The American Revolution was winding down. The British, although successful in the southern colonies, were now being harassed by guerrilla and partisan forces, which negated many of the Crown's gains there. The French Navy was for the moment dominant in the area and would soon seal the fate of King George's efforts to hold his largest outpost in the New World. It was the nail in the coffin.

The gold needed to be moved so it could be used for the benefit of a new country rising on the American continent. Nevis was too populated. He could not risk its discovery.

The men worked on. There was no thievery and there were no loose lips. The treasure was deposited in twenty different locations around the Caribbean in very isolated, safe, areas. Unless one had a map, the treasure would never be found.

The man controlling the operation from afar sat in a room alone in the headquarters of General Washington as the war raged around him. He was tired and missed his family. However, his head spun with visions and plans for this new political creation, the United States of America.

He was the only person who could tie it altogether, who knew all the locations of the treasure. He would ensure the precious metal was used to its maximum benefit.

There were many ideas floating around in his head regarding the fiscal operation of his new country. The states all had very high levels of debt from the years of fighting. He wanted the new federal government to assume these debts and institutionalize a strong central government. He also had ideas about the management of the new country's finances. All of these ideas required money.

The maps of the different locations were spread out on the table in front of him. The man smiled as he finally received word that the operation was complete. The courier had just delivered the news. Silently he folded each of the maps and put them into a leather pouch. The pouch he hid inside his jacket. It never again left his person while he was alive. He was the American commander's aide-de-camp, Alexander Hamilton.

* * *

June 28, 2018
Nassau, Bahamas

Alex sat on the deck of the bar overlooking the harbor. He was into his third vodka and did not feel a thing. Drinking was in his blood. The Russian scourge had taken hold of him recently, and he drank like a fish. He ordered another. *It's no wonder that Russian male life expectancy is so low*, he thought, and smiled. It was a full twelve years below males in the United States, primarily due to alcoholism.

Better to burn out than to fade away, he contemplated.

He was at the sailing club, where he raced small sailboats. The club was old and had memories of past glory adorning the walls. Pictures, awards, trophies, and newspaper clippings were placed throughout the premises.

The Bahamians had actually recruited him to their Olympic sailing team recently. He was that good. Sailing and treasure hunting were his passions.

Just finishing a nice weekly lunch with his fellow club members, most of them elderly, he really had nothing to do the rest of the day, so he decided to drink. He looked out across the harbor to Paradise Island. Many sailboats sat at anchor and bobbed in the sunny waves. There was a nice breeze coming off the water. He tried to enjoy the scene and the moment.

The prime minister's offer was intriguing.

Alex was the premier treasure hunter in the Caribbean. He had spent most of his adult life attempting to find and catalogue the wrecks that littered the ocean floor around the many islands and cays that formed the country known as the Bahamas. His talents were well known.

"I want to form a partnership," the prime minister had said. "You have something I want, and I have something you want."

What the man wanted was money, money in the form of gold. He knew Alex would find many treasures if he kept up his quest. There were rumors that a large find could be in the works.

Alex wanted to be free from government interference. There was the slight sticky point that the treasure Alex found technically belonged to the Bahamian people. The government always took its share and then some. In fact they could confiscate the treasure altogether. The prime minister suggested that Alex could do away with these silly worries by splitting the booty with him, illegally of course. All proceeds were to be deposited in an appropriate offshore account that did not bear his name.

Alex flagged the club waiter and ordered another drink, and stood.

Whenever he felt the stress rising through his chest, he started pacing. When he started pacing, he knew the unhappiness was coming. He stepped near the table and reached for the alcohol. It had become ingrained in him. It was the only thing that calmed the waters, the only thing that got him through the night. Sometimes, it was what got him through the day as well. He looked forward to the first drink, every day about this time. He knew it was a problem, but he shrugged it off. *There are worse problems, and I'm Russian. It's in my blood*, he thought.

The vodka went down easily. At least he had ordered the good stuff.

He looked again at the towering spires of Atlantis rising from Paradise Island across the harbor. The resort and casino brought throngs of rich Americans to the island, where they parted with their money. He casually watched as an older couple sat on the deck of their sailboat anchored one hundred yards from the club. They sipped drinks and stared back in his direction, oblivious to the machinations of the local economy. Their world was their boat and the casino behind them.

"This endeavor is becoming quite lucrative," he murmured to himself. He thought again of the prime minister.

It was an intriguing proposal indeed.

But Alex had other masters, and he had to be very careful.

* * *

May 23, 1701
London, England

The macabre parade made its way to Execution Dock, Wapping, London. Captain Kidd was tied up with several other condemned men in a horse-drawn cart with the full effects of the horror of eighteenth-century London. He was poked with sticks, urinated on, and smeared with excrement as the column weaved down the cobblestone streets to his end. He had been drinking drams of rum all morning and was roaring drunk. He was the life of the party. He bellowed at his tormentors in the crowd and gave them what they wanted, a sick scene of sadism.

What a fall he had taken. Four years ago, he had been a respected businessman and mariner who had bought a pew in Trinity Church in New York. He had a beautiful family and was respected by the Crown. Now he was a hated pirate about to die.

The procession made its way to the gallows. The birds were swarming, as they knew what was coming. This realization frightened Kidd more than anything. He tried to put the thought out of his mind.

He was to be gibbeted. In other words, his body was to be left hanging in the harbor for the birds to pick at for twenty years until all that was left was his skeleton. This would be a warning to future generations of the consequences of piracy.

Kidd had made one last plea. He told the court of his wealth hidden in the Caribbean, but unfortunately they did not believe him. "I offer you one hundred thousand pounds in gold for my freedom," he had stated. The court had laughed.

The gold therefore stayed hidden in Nevis.

Pardons arrived at the last moment, but alas Kidd was not among them. Several of the prisoners were released into the boisterous crowd, their families rejoicing. Life in eighteenth-century England was a day-to-day test of survival, especially if one was poor.

The horses pulled the cart underneath the platform where the ropes were hung. He remained defiant and dignified. The noose was put around his neck. The crowd of the pathetic London underclass numbering in the hundreds quickly became ghastly silent. This was the best part. This was their entertainment.

The cart was abruptly pulled away, and he hung briefly but tumbled to the ground. The crowd howled and rushed forward. They wanted to see the death dance as the condemned writhed under the gallows in agony, soiling their trousers.

The rope had snapped against his neck, and he had fallen.

I'm still alive, he marveled. The rope had broken.

The executioner would not be foiled a second time. The hanging was prepared again, the noose put around his neck, and the cart was pushed away. This time the rope held, and Captain Kidd died. Relatives of the other men swinging in their nooses wept as they pulled on the legs of their loved ones to hasten their death.

Sarah could not bear to be in London for Kidd's trial. She also feared for her daughter's safety in England. She waited in New York for the return of her husband. He did not arrive.

She received news of his hanging some time later.

She was ordered out of her home by the colonial government and lost all of her possessions. Despite this unfortunate outcome, she hired an attorney and fought the order; the residence was eventually returned to her.

She remarried and had another child named William. However, she outlived her fourth husband as well as her daughter. She was the only one left alive who actually knew where Kidd's treasure was located, but she never spoke of it again. Its location died with her. She passed on a very wealthy woman in spite of the treasure and left her possessions to Captain Kidd's grandchildren.

CHAPTER EIGHT

December 16, 1792
New York

The secretary of the Treasury sat back in the large, wooden chair behind the expansive desk in his office. He allowed himself a few minutes of rest and closed his eyes. He could feel the tension falling away from his face. It was a trick he had learned during the war, when he had to get sleep when he could; twenty minutes and he could be as good as new. *Funny the memories that stay with me,* he thought.

It had been a long day. The dire affairs of his new country needing immediate attention were numerous. Debts from the last wars, troubles along the frontier to pay for, and building up a new Revenue Cutter Service to protect his country from threats offshore were all on his mind. However, his heart was very troubled for a different reason.

The previous day, he had been visited by two of his colleagues in government, James Monroe and Aaron Burr. They confronted him regarding allegations that he had improperly used his influence as secretary of the Treasury, and they believed he was corrupt.

He vehemently denied these accusations, as he knew himself to be scrupulous in the affairs of state. However, he did admit that the rumors that he had been unfaithful to his wife were true.

His confession of his affair with Maria Reynolds would possibly soon be published in the local paper and would be public knowledge. It had been going on for years, and it also hurt him that he would have to tell his wife. He was to be disgraced. He described in detail to the men the carnal events that had taken place between him and the woman. That thought brought him awake again, and he sat up in the chair. *No, I have to rest*, he told himself.

He fell back again and closed his eyes. It was a battle that played out frequently with him as he drove himself in his duties; however, sometimes his body just had to take a break. He was older now.

His life was falling apart; however, there was still one thing that drove him: the financial security of his country, the country he helped birth.

After a brief respite, he opened his eyes and took a look at the maps before him spread out on the desk, twenty in all. All of the locations were in the Caribbean. They were small, out-of-the-way hiding places that no one would ever find. It had taken him years to search out these locations. He had his men then get them ready for the deposits, which soon were to be stored at each one. He was much younger at that time. He never could have moved the gold now from Nevis; the area was too populated and he was too old. He didn't have the energy anymore. But it was safe now in these hidden locations, and that thought warmed his heart.

The Bank of New York and the Bank of the United States had been established. It was time to fund them properly. The gold would do this. It was his dream, the only thing that allowed him to sleep at night, even if ever so infrequently.

The most important entity was the Bank of the United States, which had been founded the year before. Only $2 million of its initial $10 million of capital had been provided by the U.S. government. The rest was to come from private individuals. The treasure would allow the bank to grow in capability and influence, two things Hamilton knew were crucial to its success. America needed a central bank to manage its currency and ensure continuity of payments. There was a lot of opposition to the institution's having this much power, but he knew without it there would be financial chaos.

He put the maps into the leather pouch, deposited the pouch in his jacket pocket as always, and left his office.

Tomorrow he would put the final plan in motion and bring the gold home. That thought kept him going.

* * *

June 30, 2018
Nassau

They checked several more of the map locations that Connor had retrieved from the chest at the trust company in Nassau. Each foray ended in the same result, empty. The treasure had been moved. Connor was stumped. He knew in his heart that the documents he had been given were authentic. *What am I missing?* The only thing he knew to do was to return to the law offices in Nassau and go through the material with a fine-tooth comb. Alex was champing at the bit to be brought into the trust offices as well to go over the documents, but Connor refused. Money had a way of corrupting people, and he did not trust anyone that much. Besides, he was now suspicious of Alex. He dared not give away any more information.

He sat in the mahogany room at the trust company for hours poring over the items in the chest. He was amazed at the complete silence of the room and the adjoining offices. *It must be a nice life to be a trustee*, he mused. *There's been absolutely nothing happening here all day.*

He found no new information in his reexamination of the contents of the container. Exasperated, he slammed the lid to the chest down after replacing all of the documents. He was late to meet Kate. Perhaps he would never solve this puzzle. The imprint of a baby lion stared him in the face from on top of the chest. *Strange*, he thought as he made his way out of the conference room.

The receptionist let him out. He exited the building and felt the blast furnace of the heat hit him as he walked onto Bay Street in Nassau. The traffic was deadlocked as he walked between the cars to the other side of the thoroughfare. A policeman in white colonial attire attempted to direct traffic. He wondered if absent the cars it looked the same two hundred years ago. Some of the vintage drawings of the harbor showed several of the current landmarks that were still standing.

She was waiting at a little Greek restaurant that Connor frequented when in the Bahamas. It was located on the upper floor of the building lining the traffic artery through the town. The deck was crowded, but she had secured a table overlooking the hustle and bustle below. The family waitstaff was handling the crowd with their usual pleasantness.

It was late morning, and Kate was glistening in the sunlight as the sweat covered her chest and brow. Sometimes people could not beat the heat here; they just had to learn how to coexist.

Connor stopped the lump in his throat as he saw her. *I again forgot how beautiful she is*, he thought as he sat down across the small, wrought iron table.

"I love this place," he said as he eased into his chair. "I always come here when in Nassau, although usually by myself. They know me."

"I've heard that before," she responded.

They had been together on several expeditions with Alex and were now rather friendly.

"Where's your sidekick?" she asked. "I half expected him to show up with you today. It's not often a girl gets you for brunch by herself."

"He's in the office today. I thought we could maybe get to know one another better. You should feel special."

"I do," she answered. "Do you want a drink?"

"Love one."

"Two Bloody Marys," she relayed to the young Greek girl taking orders.

The realization hit Connor between the eyes, and he literally was forced back in his chair against the railing overlooking the street below.

"Oh my God," he whispered to himself.

"What's wrong, Connor?"

"It was blood on the pouch," he said aloud.

"What?"

"It was Alexander Hamilton's blood, "the Little Lion." I have been a fool and didn't see it."

"I don't understand."

"There was a baby lion imprinted on the top of the chest. Alexander Hamilton's nickname was "the Little Lion." The dark substance on the pouch was his blood from the duel. Incredible," he said softly. *Burr must have found access to the trust Hamilton had established.*

He was lost in his thoughts, taken back to the shoreline in New Jersey over two hundred years ago. He felt like he was actually there.

He downed the Bloody Mary and said, "I've got to get back to the law office. There has to be more there I'm missing."

Connor left, and Kate was somewhat annoyed.

What does that mean? Being annoyed? she asked herself. "Are you falling for him? You're not supposed to do that," she said aloud.

She finished her drink alone, paid the bill, and left.

Connor sat at the table he had left an hour earlier. There was an eagerness now that had been missing then. He had stumbled onto something of more historical significance than he had ever dreamed of.

He laid all of the documents out on the table in a very orderly way. There was the journal, many maps of Caribbean locations, trust documents, and the original pouch, which also contained papers granting the bearer access to the trust. *This is how Burr had gained access to the trust and found the maps*, he thought.

The journal was not helpful, although it was a piece of national historical treasure. It was about Aaron Burr's life after the duel. It did not explain how he gained access to the bearer documents.

He must have stolen the pouch somehow, Connor surmised.

He looked at the items spread out on the oiled mahogany table. Most were maps of small cays located throughout the Bahamas and the West Indies, but one stood out from the rest.

It was a topographical map of a volcano looming out of the ocean, which had formed an island around it. There was no name on the map, but it was obvious as to its location. "I'm going to Nevis," said Connor aloud. "The birthplace of Alexander Hamilton."

* * *

New York City

On the forty-fourth floor of a building across the city from Connor's office, another trading floor at a competitor firm buzzed with activity. Keshwar Rajim loved New York City. Since he had arrived here from India ten years ago, he had become extremely successful trading bonds. He was a natural. He could read the economic tea leaves better than anyone. He would put on trades accordingly and bring his clients in as well. He became very wealthy and had developed a devoted following. He also was very young.

Part of his success came from the fact that he had some very well-heeled clients. He could throw up some size when putting on a trade. Some of his trades were so large that he feared moving the market. It was a good problem to have.

Keshwar had been contacted years ago by an Asian businessman who wanted to set up an account. He was brand new to the business and was flattered by the opportunity. It was a lucky break for him, and he never questioned why a client of such size would seek out such an inexperienced trader.

The orders were fairly small at first but over the years had grown substantially. The funds were run through an offshore trust on the island of Nevis. He had done the due diligence on the man and the trust itself, and was comfortable he was not exposing himself or the firm legally. However, the sums had now grown quite large. He was not asking any questions. He had done his homework. He was making too much money.

Let sleeping dogs lie, he thought to himself.

Keshwar prided himself on making money for his clients. They came to him for ideas, and he had acquired a nice stable of what in the business they called "pots of money."

Currently he was shorting U.S. Treasury bonds across the yield curve. The Federal Reserve had been flooding the market for years with printed money. There was no way the Chinese or any other foreign creditor would continue to buy Treasuries at these low rates. Already there were the beginnings of stress in the new-issue auctions that came several days a week from the Fed. The tails were getting longer, and the bid-to-cover ratio was shrinking. The United States was starting to have trouble selling its debt.

In order to continue floating this astronomical debt load on the international capital markets, the U.S. would have to start paying significantly higher levels of interest. This meant that the bonds currently outstanding would be worth less and their value would drop. The Federal Reserve could not keep buying its own bonds forever to hold down interest rates. This is what Keshwar was counting on.

He could feel it. It was going to happen. It was a home run, the big short.

The debt load was now unsustainable. The U.S. was like Greece, who had defaulted several years ago, but on a scale that was unimaginable. There was no way the United States could pay back the debt. The economic power of the world had shifted east to Asia. It was people like Keshwar who recognized this and were planning to become rich off this realization.

The Bloomberg terminal squawked with an incoming message. Most trading was done this way now, as there was a written record of the conversation as opposed to verbal communication, which introduced additional human error.

The market data terminal system, or Bloomberg, was founded and developed by the now multibillionaire Michael Bloomberg of New York City fame in the early eighties. He presciently had realized that Wall Street would pay big for a terminal system that could provide fast, accurate market data, along with associated analytics. Over the years, a messaging service was added, which recorded all trading communication and currently was relied on to provide proof of instructions given. Trading systems were standard to the system now as well.

With over 250,000 terminals presently in the network worldwide, the business was a cash cow. The monthly access fee was not cheap. One could not realistically operate on Wall Street today without a Bloomberg.

The orders were transmitted briefly and succinctly. Keshwar sold another hundred million U.S. long-term bonds for his client.

* * *

July 1, 2018

"You like her a lot, don't you?" asked Alex as Kate's car drove up to the club.

"I do, mate; she's special," said Connor as he glanced in the direction of Alex's gaze.

Kate drove up the hill to the parking lot and was now walking higher towards the building, where the two sat nursing a couple of beers on the upper deck. They watched her slowly approach. It was a pleasant sight.

The Cricket Club overlooked the Bahamas National Cricket field in Nassau. The downstairs level consisted of locker rooms for the home and opposing teams. The second floor was comprised of a bar and restaurant with a large deck, which allowed patrons to eat and drink and have a perfect view of the field. It was a very British scene with a touch of Caribbean thrown in for spice. The wall around the field was covered in pastel advertisements that the area was known for.

Cricket had its roots in the early medieval bat-and-ball games of Europe. It was derived from the same origin as American baseball. The two games evolved along different lines but from the same general source, similar to the evolution of man and apes from the same origin. The name "cricket" was believed to come from the Old English word "cricc," which meant "staff" or "rod." Cricket became very well established in England as the national sport, and then spread throughout the English-speaking colonies with the growth of the British Empire. In the Caribbean, cricket was worshipped and created great nationalistic fervor.

The game consisted of a bowler pitching the ball toward a batsman. The batsman had to hit the ball and run to touch the crease at the other end of a rectangular pitch in order to score a run. Outfielders similar to baseball's fielded the ball and tried to dismiss the batsman. The game was played on an oval field and could last for up to five days. As an American, Connor did not understand the passion the game created in-country, but he was attempting to learn the sport.

Above the field stood Fort Charlotte perched on the high ground. Her cannons pointed outward towards the harbor a quarter mile away to the north, as they had done hundreds of years before. It was as if they still protected the island from invaders. The cruise ships were moving in and out of the harbor as always. The sun was making its way down to the horizon, accentuating the crystal-clear blue water. A cool breeze took the edge off the heat as the night approached.

Kate walked through the bar and restaurant area on the upper floor and joined them both on the deck. Connor pulled up a metal chair for her as she arrived, the feet of the chair screeching over the surface of the floor.

"Well I can see you both are doing well at the moment," she said as she surveyed the multiple empty Boddingtons on the table.

"Yes, several dead soldiers," responded Alex. He motioned for the waitress to bring another round.

They drank for a couple of hours in the pleasant Bahamian environment. Several of the local girls came up to Alex, and he slipped them money under the table. They walked away embarrassed but happy. Kate and Connor shot him inquisitive glances.

"I cover the health insurance for a few of the local ladies I've met here over the years," he remarked. "Sometimes you have to give back a little, you know?"

"Ah, so you have a soft spot," remarked Kate. She was getting to know him better but still had reservations. "You really have gone native."

"You have no idea," Alex fired back. The banter between them was awkward, thought Connor. It was obvious Alex didn't like her.

They enjoyed the early evening.

Sometime later, a younger, native black man approached the table. Connor saw Alex stiffen.

"You need to be careful, Alex," the man said in a thick Bahamian accent. "You need to protect ya tings, mon," he said again in broken Caribbean English.

"You need to watch what you sayin', mon, in front of my friends," Alex shot back.

Alex stood up out of his chair to face the man, and they stared each other down. Kate put her hand on Connor's leg as they looked at each other, wondering what was going on.

"You gonna get hurt, mon. We know what you're bein up to."

"Leave," Alex commanded. "Before I hurt you myself."

The man turned away and went down the stairs out of the club.

"Something you want to tell me?" asked Connor when the guy was out of sight.

"My business, mon."

"No problem," Connor answered, but he was worried.

Connor and Kate left the club, and she drove them both back to the Hilton. The Bahamian nightlife was still raging around them as they walked from the parking lot to the lobby. They ended up sitting in the bar late into the evening. Their company was a group of English flight attendants who had flown in that night. Obviously they weren't flying the next day, as they were drinking heavily.

Since Alex had left for the evening to go home, Kate asked, "So what's going on with your friend?"

"I don't know but something is definitely going down. I'm worried," Connor answered.

"That's an understatement. He's crashing and burning, and you don't know why."

"He's a friend and I trust him. Or at least I used to."

"Well maybe you shouldn't."

They stared at each other for an eternity.

"Speaking of crashing, why don't you just crash in my room," Connor offered. "I've got a king and I won't take advantage of you," he teased, and winked at her.

She looked at him with a discerning eye for a few moments.

"Maybe I'll take you up on that," she responded. "No reason to pay for another room this late at night." *What the hell, I like him*, she thought.

They made their way to the elevator.

CHAPTER NINE

July 2, 2018

The fire leaped out of the window in the tower directly across from him like a tongue; he saw people in the window nearby actually incinerated in the fireball. Smoke was pouring out of all the openings above the eightieth floor like water from a colander. He could feel the terror. It consumed him. It was as if it controlled him, played with him.

He searched each of the windows from the top of the building down until he saw her. She was calling for him, looking for him desperately with her eyes. She couldn't find him.

The fire came closer; she began to cry in pain.

Another man from the same office was next to her. He reached out and held her hand. The windows had long blown out, sending the glass to endanger anyone left standing below. They looked at each other in sorrow and accepted their fate. They jumped.

"No!" Connor screamed.

He shot up in the bed and emptied his lungs in unbearable horror.

Kate awoke in a frightful state, trying to understand where she was. She was disoriented. She was in a strange environment.

When she realized it was Connor, she reached for him. She pulled him close and covered him with kisses.

"It's okay," she said quietly over and over again. "I'm here, I'm here. Shhhhh."

Connor was shaking. Slowly he started to calm down.

She pushed him back down on the bed and straddled him. He tried to say something, but she held her hand to his mouth. She pulled off the T-shirt she was wearing and bent down and kissed him, softly at first but then harder. Her breasts lightly touched his chest teasingly.

Connor responded violently, pulling her close to him. He reached down and ripped off her panties and entered her. She whimpered softly. They made love for what seemed like an eternity.

He exploded inside of her as she cried out in pleasure. Neither one of them said anything for a long time. Then Connor broke the silence.

"My wife died in the Twin Towers. I've haven't been with another woman since," he said softly as she lay next to him and caressed his face.

* * *

The next morning, Connor found himself walking along the man-made boardwalk lining the shore of the harbor in Nassau. The pounding surf had eaten away at the concrete barrier, and parts were falling into the ocean. The sea constantly tried to change the islands, and the humans constantly tried to stop it.

It's a never-ending battle, he thought.

His heart was heavy. He was confused.

Kate had left early on her way back to the science institute on Eleuthera.

He had emptied his heart to her. He hoped it wasn't too much for her, but she seemed like she really cared. He had connected with her.

He loved Emily very much. Up until the day he met his wife, he had not really felt love. She filled a hole that was unfillable.

He picked up a rock and threw it into the crystal-clear blue water. It was beautiful here. The morning air was clean and crisp, but the heat was coming.

He wanted the pain to stop but didn't know how. Kate seemed to show the way out, but could he trust her? The age-old problem: does he open himself up to someone and the possibility of her not living up to his expectations or to the possibility of losing her as well? It was unfair of him to hold her to that standard.

He kept walking. The local kids were playing in the surf and laughing with their parents. A naked baby girl played in the waves.

That should have been my life, he thought angrily.

Suddenly he realized he was feeling guilty. He had been with another woman besides his wife.

He reached the other side of the park near the harbor and saw the line of bars highlighted with pastel Caribbean colors. Breakfast was cooking and alcohol was available. The smell of conches cooking on the fire drew him closer.

"Time for a drink," he said to himself as he walked to the nearest hut.

* * *

April 23, 1804
New York

Aaron Burr was seething with rage, the kind of rage that can turn a heart cold.

He stared at the election results.

He had lost again. He had worked so hard to achieve the pinnacle of success, yet it had eluded him once more. He was still not satisfied. The ambition burned within him.

His political career was basically over. This time it was the governorship of New York that had slipped through his fingers. He couldn't believe it. He didn't want to believe it. He threw the newspaper across the room.

Previously it was the presidency of the United States. He had been tied in the Electoral College with Thomas Jefferson. He was running as Jefferson's vice presidential candidate. Although he did not ask to be moved to the top of the ticket, things worked out so that he could have been elected. His supporters had made it possible for him to be president.

But then Hamilton's Federalist Party prevented Burr's election to the presidency. It was a bitter pill to swallow.

Jefferson never forgave him for getting that close, even though it was not Burr's intention.

Then a second term as vice president was taken from him. Jefferson did not want him on the ticket a second time. He was still angry about Burr's having challenged him for his first term. Burr actually was very loyal to Jefferson and a sterling ruler of the Senate, but it was all for naught. Even many of his political opponents had voiced appreciation for his evenhanded oversight of the upper chamber of the United States Congress.

So he had run for governor of New York. This time a smear campaign by the current governor, Clinton, did the trick to defeat him.

There was a common cause running through all of these defeats: Alexander Hamilton. His conniving and intrigue directed against Burr was unfortunately very effective. He called Burr "a dangerous man, and one who ought not be trusted with the reins of government."

The end result was that Aaron Burr was shut out of national political office.

To make things worse, Hamilton was out gallivanting all over town and disgracing Burr's good name. Burr was hearing many reports of comments made or disparagement thrown in his direction by the miscreant. This would not stand.

Hamilton was quoted at a recent political dinner saying "that he could express a still-more-despicable opinion of Burr."

Burr challenged Hamilton for an explanation, but Hamilton only mocked him in the local press. He pretended to give Burr a lesson in the proper use of the English language.

"My honor will be avenged," Burr said aloud to himself. The anger burned within him. It almost reached the level of his ambition.

It is time to stop playing by the rules. I have been a loyal, gallant military officer, and Washington spurned me. Jefferson turned against me. Hamilton has questioned my honor. Yes, it is time to change the rules. I will kill him!

He would challenge Hamilton to a duel.

* * *

July 3, 2018

Connor returned to the Hilton after his walk ready for a nap after five beers at the bar. He had attempted to drink his problems away, but as always they lurked somewhere in the back of his mind, occasionally making themselves heard through the alcoholic haze with a vengeance.

He entered the hotel lobby and noticed the mural of Nassau's history emblazoned high on the far wall. His thoughts turned back to Hamilton. *How did Burr acquire access to the trust?* he thought. The answers eluded him. *I need to get to Nevis. There I will find what I am looking for. I can feel it.*

Upon entering his room, he picked up his phone and dialed a friend. Oliver picked up the phone; the accent was unmistakable.

"Oliver, it's Connor. I'm sorry to call you so late in the day."

"Hello, Connor, don't be silly," Oliver remarked in his aristocratic English accent. "It's a beautiful day here in Geneva. I have to say you are the last person I thought I would hear from today!" His cheerfulness came through the phone as always.

Oliver was an elderly currency trader, who had made his fortune in London and then moved to Switzerland years ago. Connor had traded with him extensively in the past and knew him quite well, although they had never met in person.

For decades Oliver had spent many months a year in Nevis at his home on the side of the mountain. Connor had stayed at the villa many times over the years free of charge. It was one of the fringe benefits of having wealthy clients.

Calling it a home was an understatement. It was a stately compound built in the Caribbean style, perched on the side of the dormant volcano. The view was magnificent.

There was the main house plus two cottages and a terrace with a pool. The outdoor kitchen next to the swimming area allowed for a view of the jungle to the side of the terrace. Of course the entire home was staffed with cooks, maids, and other hired help. It was lovely—magical, in fact.

Oliver had become a fixture on the island and was quite well liked by the locals.

"I need to borrow your home on Nevis for a period of time. Is it being used?"

"Why no, my boy, I have not been able to get there very much in my advanced years. My wife is quite sick, as well you know. Of course you can use it. I'll have the caretaker contact you and make the arrangements."

"Thank you, Oliver. Tell me something. Do you know anything about Alexander Hamilton?"

"Ahh," said Oliver. There was a short silence and then he spoke again. "Why do you ask that, Connor?"

"I'm chasing a myth."

"You're looking for gold?"

Startled, Connor responded, "Yes, how did you know?" His surprise came through in his voice.

"It's been rumored for many centuries that Alexander Hamilton had a treasure trove on the island somewhere. People have looked for it over and over again. No one has ever found it."

"Well it's true," said Connor. "I can prove it."

"Indeed, you must enlighten me sometime."

"Well maybe when we finally meet in person. Where do I start my search?"

"I would start with an ancient woman named Alma. She's a native and must be over a hundred years old at this point. There was a myth out there that she knew something about this issue from her family, but she just talks gibberish. Maybe you could start there on your quest."

"Thanks, Oliver. I hope your wife feels better and you get to see your beautiful home again."

"So do I Connor, so do I."

"Good-bye, my friend."

Connor hung up the phone and then called his assistant to start making travel arrangements.

CHAPTER TEN

April 23, 1803

Alexander Hamilton was tired. He had lived a full life. For some reason, he had a foreboding that he might be near the end of that life. He was all right with this feeling. He accepted it.

There was a sadness about him as well. His oldest and beloved son, Phillip, had been killed in a duel, mainly as a result of Hamilton's political conflicts. His older daughter had suffered a nervous breakdown because of his son's death and really never recovered. He missed them both.

Combined with the destruction of his reputation due to the revelations of his affair with Maria Reynolds, these stresses had darkened his life. Of course his relationship with his wife was strained as well. There was no one to confide in anymore. He felt alone.

However, he believed he had accomplished many things, which he had, of course. He felt at peace for the first time that he could remember. He just had a few more details to put in order, and then he could accept whatever the future held.

The trip from New York to the Bahamas did not take as long as he had expected, less than two weeks. It was uneventful. The weather and therefore the sea was calm, and the wind was steady. He had actually enjoyed the voyage down the American coast. The open air had done him good. His spirits were lifted somewhat.

Upon arrival into Nassau Harbor, he was greeted by a long oar boat and rowed into town as prearranged. He arrived in the Bahamas anonymously.

He checked in to the main hotel downtown and then was driven by carriage immediately to the law offices of one of the prominent firms in Nassau that had been in existence for some years now. This also had been prearranged. He suspected he would feel anxiety performing this chore, but to his delight, he felt only calm.

In his mind, this location was perfect. It was out of his country and in a place where his detractors in the United States would never guess. The British legal system was famous for its rule of law. His secrets would be safe here, even though it was obvious there would eventually be another war between America and Britain. And secrets they were, secrets that people and governments would kill for. They were keys to a treasure beyond belief.

Remarkably, Hamilton had always been a fan of Great Britain and its governmental system. A strong central government was important to him. He thought it necessary for his new country to become the world power that was rightfully hers. Now the British rule of law would help foster the rise of the United States. The irony was remarkable.

It only took a few hours to set up the trust. It was created as a bearer trust, meaning whoever presented the appropriate documents physically to the trustees would be granted access.

He was led into a room and given some privacy.

He had carried these documents on him now for years, and it would be hard to let them go, although it was a relief. If something happened to him now, there would be a mechanism for him to transfer the knowledge to someone of his choosing.

The small, fine, wooden chest given to him had been engraved per his instructions. A little lion glared at him from the top of the polished box. He smiled. It was a nice touch. He thought briefly of his childhood in Nevis. It brought joy to his heart, something he had been missing for some time now. He thought of his friend, the slave girl. Little did he understand at the time how that day on the mountain with her would change the course of history.

His thoughts drifted to the political battles raging in the United States. Hamilton had been in a quandary. *What to do with this wealth?*

He had despised Adams and worked to defeat him for a second presidential term. Hamilton thought he was too emotional and impulsive to be trusted with power any longer. He also despised Jefferson.

Hamilton was a Federalist. He believed in an economy directed by the government based on manufacturing and guided by the elite to compete on the world stage. Jefferson supported states' rights and an agrarian economy. He supported the French Revolution. The people knew best for themselves, Jefferson believed, and he feared a strong central government.

Hamilton knew what he had to do. He could not entrust such a large sum of money to someone who did not agree with his theories on how government should be established and run.

So he had to wait. He had to wait until the government changed, when Jefferson and Adams were long gone. Then he could turn over the gold to the U.S. Treasury and rest in peace.

He deposited the documents one last time in the chest and then closed the lid and locked it per the trustee's instructions. The bearer beneficiary documents he put in a leather pouch, and he stowed the pouch in his jacket. Then he exited the room, gave the key to the trustee, and made his way back to the hotel.

Now he could let go of the stress; the information was safe and there was a mechanism for succession of his secrets.

He stayed in Nassau until the next ship left for New York, which was several weeks. He barely left his room. He did, however, make several excursions around the island. He always loved to understand the history and culture of places he visited.

The cruise back to New York was uneventful.

* * *

July 3, 2018
Nassau, Bahamas

Alex looked nervously in the mirror behind him as he drove. The headlights had disappeared. He relaxed briefly, but only briefly. It had looked menacingly like he was being followed. Now he was the only car on the road.

He was playing a dangerous game.

He pulled off the road violently and drove into a driveway where he could be hidden. The stucco wall surrounding the property shielded him from the street. He was breathing heavily, and he gripped the steering wheel like a steel clamp.

Calm down, he told himself. He relaxed his hands.

He just had to make sure. He waited.

The payoff to his game was obvious. There was money to be gained from the deal with the prime minister, and he wanted money. However, the payoff from his other efforts was on a much grander scale. Alex had an axe to grind, a wrong to right.

His thoughts briefly drifted back to his parents, but he immediately pushed them out of his mind. It only made him angry.

Not now, he told himself. *Focus!*

There was no one on the road.

This time, they are not following me. Next time maybe I won't be so lucky, he thought.

He pulled out of his hiding place and continued down the thoroughfare on the way into Nassau.

The thugs working for the prime minister had been making their point. They did not want him withholding the information on the treasure he was seeking. The prime minister did not like to be made out to be a fool. It was becoming obvious to them that Alex was not cooperating fully. They were unsophisticated but effective in their methods. And Alex was an easy target.

The previous morning they had explained their position very effectively by physically threatening him. Two large men had caught him walking to his car early in the morning outside of his house on the way to work. They were waiting for him. One had a crowbar and threatened to use it on his face. Alex was a sitting duck while he remained in the Bahamas.

He actually liked his jaw and didn't want it broken. He unconsciously touched his chin.

However, his other masters were much more long-term oriented. They were the really scary ones. The ones he didn't want to piss off.

He would play cat and mouse with the natives for a while and earn some money while he took care of his other obligations.

* * *

Nevis

The ride from the airport to Oliver's house was spectacular, especially for someone who had never been on the island, like Kate.

A small aircraft had flown them in from St. Lucia an hour before and carried only twelve people. The flight was quick but bumpy as the wind played its games with the tiny prop-engine plane, or "bug-smasher," as Connor called it. He was happy when they were safe on the ground and were taxiing to the small building.

The runway was carved into the base of the volcano, a long strip only a few meters above the sea. It formed a demarcation between the rolling sea and the towering mountain.

The airport terminal was more like a shack than anything else. Outside, the drivers waited and hoped to pick up a paying fare. Stray dogs mingled with the baggage stacked under the overhang beyond the entrance. Tropical vines grew up the side of the structure, their flowers blowing in the breeze as they looked up at the sun. Kate took in the aroma as they waited.

Connor had called ahead for transportation. It was late, of course.

The taxi that finally picked them up from the airport was an old Volkswagen van that was held together with paper clips, it seemed to Connor. The driver was very friendly and helped store their bags in the rear compartment and then opened the sliding door. Cold beer from the local brewery and bottled water awaited them inside. They were on their way.

They wound around the base of the old volcano and thirty minutes later passed through the capital of Charlestown. The local foliage covered the road overhead in some places, while at other times the road was naked against the ocean. The waves bounded up the seawall and threatened to attack the vehicle. Avoiding the potholes and oncoming traffic on the small, semipaved road seemed more an art than a science.

Soon they reached the capital. The downtown area was bustling with natives; a few tourists and businessmen mingled among them. They wore collared shirts and ties but no jackets.

Although the buildings were decrepit, the town was full of life and commerce. It had been this way for hundreds of years. The ferries were offloading supplies and passengers at the harbor terminal. The locals hung out on the street corners and wasted time as the laughing, uniformed schoolchildren congregated on the way home. *Nothing ever changes here*, thought Connor as they drove through the town.

Kate leaned into him in the backseat of the taxi. It had been a long day flying in from New York. They both were tired but the scenery was beautiful. She snuggled up into him and put her head on his shoulder. Connor looked down at her and she smiled. They were happy.

He was scared to enjoy the feeling. He didn't trust that it would last.

They drove upwards now towards the rim of the dormant volcano, passing the markets on the outskirts of town. Passing the old cemetery, the drive became more hazardous. The vegetation grew thicker, and the streets became narrower and more dangerous. Monkeys flew from tree to tree as they drove higher up the incline. At times there was space for only one vehicle, and they had to pull over to let oncoming traffic pass. Villages came and went as they climbed higher and higher.

Finally, after about forty-five minutes, they reached a level parking area two-thirds of the way up the mountain after many twists and turns. The taxi driver pulled into the small space carved into the rock and stopped the van. Connor and Kate climbed out and turned to look at the view.

"Wow," she said.

The island rolled down the mountain before them as the lush vegetation covered most everything in a shade of bright green. The contrast of the colors against the deep blue sea was breathtaking. The scene was speckled with homes sticking out of the trees and then turned into a sea of rooftops as the viewer gazed on Charlestown guarding the harbor. St. Kitts rose out of the dark blue ocean beyond, a short ferry ride away. She was a multipeaked island and much more expansive than Nevis. The Eastern Caribbean Central Bank was located there, controlling the currency for the Eastern Caribbean region.

"I could get used to this place," Kate said teasingly as she followed the taxi driver into the house carrying the bags, as the housekeeper showed him the way to the main cabana.

Connor strolled out onto the deck and took in the view.

* * *

The Asian man had rented the house several days before. He paid cash. There were no questions asked, as he paid three times the usual price for the time period. The tourist trade was operating well below normal, so the owners didn't balk at the man's request for privacy; they were just happy to have a renter.

The home had an expansive tile deck jutting out from the mountain. A waist-high stone railing guarded the precipice overlooking the incline down the mountain below. Since the dormant volcano was the only tall structure on the island, the view was unencumbered. The deck teemed with life as the various species of native reptiles scurried and scratched across the open space and along the wall, creating a racket of their own.

To the rear of deck was an open veranda. The light wooden screens were the only thing that could keep out the elements and were easily closed. The property fit the Asian man's needs perfectly, because it overlooked the house on the mountain below him and to the left. He spent his first day on the island outfitting that empty house with listening devices in each room and in the phones. The structure was easily broken into, as it had not been rented or occupied in some time. He also set up a sophisticated camera with a high-powered telephoto lens on the deck trained on the object of interest. Then all he had to do was wait.

Now his target had arrived, but he was not alone as he had hoped.

Connor walked out on the expansive stone patio at Oliver's home, and the man started taking pictures.

* * *

December 12, 1805
Nassau, Bahamas

He missed South Carolina. This surprised him. He had always considered the Northeast home.

But there was something about the South. Something he liked. Maybe it was the way the moss hung from the trees, or the way the women talked. *Yes, it must be the women*, he thought. It was always the women. Anyway, he liked it.

Of course the main thing he missed was Theodosia. His daughter was the most beautiful thing in his life. His wife had died early in their marriage, so it was Burr who had raised the child. He made her into a prodigy. She was groomed to be elite, above the rest. Fluent in multiple languages and schooled in the cultures of the world, she was a prize for her new husband in South Carolina, the governor. He also desperately loved her.

The capital came into view. The Bahamian capital, Nassau, that is.

The trip down from Georgetown, South Carolina, had been rough. The weather had not been on his side for the voyage, but he had made it. He was here.

And here was the answer to his dreams.

Perhaps it was the fact that his parents had died at an early age. Perhaps it was the multiple frustrations in his life. Washington had not given him the proper recognition during the war. He had been denied the presidency and the governorship of New York. Who knew what it was, but Aaron Burr had ambition. It was a driving force burning within him. It drove him to achieve the pinnacle of success. It also drove him to do stupid things.

He reached into his coat to tap the pouch that was hidden inside, just to make sure it was still there. It was. He breathed a small sigh of relief as he folded up his collar to protect himself from the cold wind off the ocean. He hadn't realized the Bahamas was this cold this time of year.

Now he could make his aspirations, finally, come true. He was so close, he could taste it. This money would allow him to fulfill his destiny.

The ship slowly made its way into port.

He boarded at one of the inns along the main thoroughfare.

Several years earlier, many loyalist families had immigrated to the Bahamas from the United States. They brought their slaves and proceeded to make a life in the islands. The atmosphere of the town was quite nice actually, he thought, almost civilized. He tried to keep a low profile among the English subjects. After all, he had killed many British soldiers in his time.

The next morning he made his way to the law offices described in the documents in the pouch. A lawyer himself, Burr understood the formalities of these arrangements and believed he could make this transaction happen. Besides, it was unlikely that anyone here knew of the events the year before in Weehawken, New Jersey.

He walked into the offices unannounced and asked for the senior partner.

He was led into an ornate boardroom with pilasters lining the walls and bookshelves filled to the ceiling. The partner arrived exactly ten minutes later. Burr introduced himself and produced the trust bearer documents.

Without a moment's hesitation, the gentleman left the room and returned a short while later bearing a small wooden chest. A golden little lion was inlaid into the wood at the top of the chest. The partner produced a key and then excused himself and left the room. Burr sat there staring at the lion for a while and then inserted the key and unlocked the chest.

His heart jumped as he saw what was inside—maps, many of them. They told of buried treasure.

CHAPTER ELEVEN

Nevis

Connor and Kate sat at an outdoor wrought iron table overlooking a beautiful Caribbean garden. Behind them sat the main house of an old sugar mill plantation, since turned into a wonderfully cozy inn situated above Charlestown on the side of the mountain. The old kettles and boilers encased in limestone dotted the landscape around the main house along with several windmills in the distance. Bougainvillea shrubs and poinsettias as big as trees dominated the hundreds of other flowers and multiple species of colorful vegetation sprinkled throughout the grounds, a very romantic setting. The sun was setting over the ocean.

Here I am with this beautiful woman in this amazing place. I'm a lucky man, thought Connor. I wonder if I am falling in love.

They had just finished dinner and were enjoying a drink in the warm evening. Again Connor was struck by the history here, the birthplace of Alexander Hamilton. He could almost take himself back in time over two hundred years and imagine the view from their location. *Probably not so different than it looks now*, he thought.

Sugar production had ruled the world at that time. The European capitals demanded the sweet substance in great amounts for their coffees and cakes. The Caribbean was the sugar production hub of the world due to the perfect climate, growing conditions, and ready-made labor force. The imported African slave population ensured the fields were always manned. Over time the slaves would become a bigger crop than the cane for the North American plantations.

The Spanish, French, English, as well as Dutch had fought over and exploited the region for several hundred years. The Caribbean was dotted with ruins of old mills and plantations from Jamaica to Barbados. The pirate trade had flourished as well, feasting on the laden cargo ships making their way from the region to all the capitals of the world. It was a glorious time.

The sun had made its way below the horizon, and the two of them retired to the bar area near the library of the inn. Shelves of antique books lined the walls, interspersed with colonial artifacts. They ordered another drink. The room was filled with tourists and businessmen staying a few nights at the inn as well as locals enjoying an evening out. It was an Ernest Hemingway moment.

Kate noticed a couple from South Africa by their unmistakable accent as well as a group of English bankers working at a local institution. But what caught her eye was an Asian man in his thirties occasionally stealing glances at them from across the bar. He looked out of place. She might have passed it off as a representative from China here on business. The Chinese were making large investments and loans in the Caribbean in order to increase their influence in the region. Many of the small sovereign governments were going to China for funds instead of accessing the public capital markets or to the multinational institutions, as the cost of doing so was prohibitive. The strings attached were also much more onerous.

The conversation went on with the South African couple for some time before Kate noticed the Asian man leave the bar and step quietly outside into the now black night.

She turned back to Connor. "I feel at home here."

He pulled her close and kissed her hair. She felt warm and inviting. Connor let his guard down another notch.

They strolled arm in arm up the winding, small, potholed road that led up to the landing in front of Oliver's house. It was such a nice evening and the inn was so close that they decided to walk. The monkeys chattered incessantly at the intruders, and the bats flew silently overhead.

Kate stopped in the night close to the house and pulled Connor close under the stars.

"I'm really glad I came here with you," she said softly, and kissed him. He responded.

They both were excited. The full moon beamed down from overhead.

"Let's get inside," said Connor with a wink, and took her by the hand.

She saw the light first, the quick flash of a small beam inside. Someone was already inside the home.

"I see it too," said Connor quietly.

He slipped up to the window where the flash had been and slowly looked inside. He could barely make out a dark shape walking through the main room, looking throughout each storage space as if he were planning to rob the place. Drawers and cabinets were being silently searched. The penlight flashed briefly from time to time as the intruder methodically went about his task.

Connor crept slowly down the walkway along the plate glass in order to get a better look in the moonlight at the situation. As he did so, one of the monkeys jumped off the roof across his back and scampered into the yard. The abrupt motion startled Connor and caused him to lash out at the animal, and he accidentally hit the glass. The monkey shrieked. The intruder turned at the noise.

He saw Connor through the dark window easily reflected against the moonlit sky. He pulled his weapon and fired high over Connor's head. The glass shattered. Connor hit the floor, and the shards rained down around him.

Immediately Kate drew a Beretta 9mm handgun from her purse and burst her way into the house. The man was making his way out of the veranda opening covered by multiple carved wooden screens.

She hit the lights and took up the classic Weaver stance with the handgun: one hand around the pistol grip and seated in the palm of the other hand. Both arms were locked, and her feet were spread wide as she crouched and fired. The bullet splattered against the tiled outdoor grill across the wide-open space, and the intruder was able to escape by leaping across the masonry wall and diving into the jungle below—however, not before she saw his face; it was the Asian man from the bar.

Connor tried to understand what had just happened as he jumped up and ran inside, his eyes adjusting to the light. Kate was still holding her weapon as she slowly made her way to the spot where the intruder had jumped, and carefully looked over the side, her weapon at the ready. She was obviously well trained.

"He's gone," she said, and turned to Connor, lowering the pistol.

"Who are you?" said a shocked Connor with an incredulous look on his face.

"I'm sorry, Connor, I lied to you. I'm an agent of the U.S. government, Treasury Department specifically. And I know about the gold."

Connor's jaw dropped. "You'd better start talking right now!" he demanded.

"You're not the only one looking for it. I'm trying to find out who that is."

"You lied to me. Everything you said was a lie."

"No! Not everything."

He stared at her in disbelief but said nothing.

"Look, we know a foreign government is attempting to find the gold or to find out if it exists. We were tipped off from an asset in the Bahamas that you had somehow found access to it and were attempting to locate it. That's when I came in."

"So you set me up! You showed up at the cabana in Eleuthera and hoped I'd come on to you."

"Yes, and if you hadn't, I would've come on to you."

"So it's all a fake?"

"No, Connor, it's not. The problem is I've fallen in love with you, which is against all of the rules."

"Yeah, save that for your next target!" he said angrily. "I opened up to you." The silence was brutal. "What do we do about this situation?" he asked a few moments later.

"Well I'm going to report in, get someone here to repair this glass, and have a drink. Want to join me?" she asked.

Connor didn't answer the question. "Who do you think is after the gold, and why are they after me?" he retorted.

"I don't know. I suspect the Chinese have some involvement, but we can't be sure at this point. We are trying to find out why they have interest as well, beyond the obvious financial motivations."

Connor walked silently alone out onto the veranda, leaving Kate in the main room of the house. The anger boiled up inside of him but was soon replaced with sorrow. *I knew she was too good to be true. I knew it!* After a few moments deciding what he should do, Connor walked back into the large, open-air room where Kate sat silently.

"I'm going to bed," said Connor wearily. "You can sleep on the couch."

* * *

January 10, 1807
Territory of Orleans

Aaron Burr slammed the newspaper down on the tavern table, making a loud sound. It had not been a good week. His men, however, didn't notice. They were too busy enjoying themselves with the girls for hire at the saloon. Music was blaring and the ale was flowing. The night was degenerating into debauchery.

Let them have fun, he thought. It had been a rough few weeks in the wilderness.

Burr had led a small group of his men into a nearby town for a little rest and relaxation. They deserved the time off from training his army.

He had searched almost every one of the locations that was provided by Hamilton's maps, which were still safely stored in the trust in the Bahamas. None proved to be holding the gold. There was only one location left, and he had dispatched a trusted colleague to comb the site several weeks back.

He had just received word the night before that it too was empty. "It has been moved," he said aloud. "Damn that Hamilton!" His dream of funding his new kingdom out west was dashed.

And now this new wrinkle; his attention drifted back to the newspaper. President Jefferson had issued a warrant for his arrest for the crime of treason. His supposed confidant General Wilkinson had betrayed him and his dreams to the president. They were to have joined forces against the Spanish with the goal of conquering the Spanish lands for themselves. The general was now waiting for him in New Orleans with his men to arrest him. Burr had been a fool to trust him.

The arrest warrant was printed in the paper. Now everyone would know and he would be a wanted man. His world and his dreams were crumbling before his eyes.

Now the only thing left to do is to get drunk, he told himself. He ordered another ale and waved to a pretty girl alone at the bar.

Nevis

Connor left the house in midmorning; Kate had gone for a run. Breakfast had been quiet and tense as they sipped coffee together on the veranda overlooking the harbor.

Connor was hurt he had been lied to. He felt Alex was right; he didn't know her. He felt used and didn't know what to do. The problem was that he was so attracted to her. No, it was more than that. He was in love with her. But now he questioned her motivation and feelings. All of this made Connor confused and angry.

The drive down the mountain was as dangerous as ever. This time it wasn't the monkeys that were the problem, even as they screamed at him. It was as if they were saying, "I told you so!"

It was the goats.

They walked into the road frequently in front of him, sometimes causing him to stop the car altogether. It was maddening.

Okay relax, mate, this isn't New York, he thought. You're wound so tight even they would think you're stressed, he said to himself. Stop and smell the roses a bit. Enjoy the goats. He laughed aloud.

It always amazed him as he passed the local businesses and roadside shacks that passed as bars how simple life was here. They survived day to day and had no idea of the world around them or how poorly they lived. *Maybe they are lucky*, he pondered. He paid particular attention to the motor scooters that flew by him on the dangerous road with no care in the world.

I guess they haven't enacted helmet laws here yet, he mused.

He arrived at the shoreline in about fifteen minutes and turned left along the coastal road, which snaked around the circular island. Again, the ancient sugar mills dotted the landscape intermixed with the clapboard shacks, which housed the natives. He believed it was the ultimate Caribbean destination. The great old windmills built to grind the cane were magnificent.

After reaching the opposite side of the island, he turned back up the mountain on a winding dirt road. He was on his way to meet Alma.

The road was much worse than what they had faced on the drive in from the airport. Maybe it wasn't even really a road but more of a wide, rocky path. The small SUV he had rented bounced its way up the uneven slope. *I'll be lucky if I don't crack an axle*, Connor thought.

Eventually he reached a plateau on the side of the ancient volcano about a mile up the slope. It allowed him to pull off the road and park. A string of shanties made of tin and scrap wood were lined up along the level area facing the ocean. Open fires and iron kettles adorned the small strip of land in front of the cottages. The locals were always cooking something. The smell was overpowering.

He had learned of Alma's whereabouts from, of all places, the help hired to clean Oliver's house. The two maids had been only too helpful in giving him specific instructions. Alma was a well-known entity on the island and almost a homegrown tourist attraction with her constant discussions of the "treasure."

"Lay dem talk," one of the maids had yelled at him as he left Oliver's home. Her belly bounced as she laughed heartily. He had smiled at her.

Connor exited the car and walked over to the last cottage on the row; the multicolored pastels were a constant reminder he was in the Caribbean, no matter how rickety the dwellings were.

Several of the half-naked kids saw him and ran to announce his arrival. *I guess this doesn't happen very often*, he thought. *Or then again maybe it does.*

An old man slowly walked to the door and beckoned him in. It was obvious what Connor was looking for. Connor stepped into the dwelling, and the boards creaked under his feet. The smells of body odor and fish boiling washed over him. He was led into the rear of the cottage past the makeshift kitchen and into a small room, which backed into the mountain.

She sat on a rocking chair in the rear of the room. A woolen blanket was draped over her, even though the temperature was close to ninety.

"She gets cold," the old man muttered to no one.

Connor turned and looked at the old woman.

"So you've finally come," she mumbled to herself before she even looked at him.

She raised her head.

Even that required a Herculean effort. She was very old. Connor couldn't even guess her age. But he did know one thing: she did not have much time left on this earth.

Her eyes took a while to focus. "I've been waiting for you."

She smiled a warm, knowing smile.

Connor walked over and sat beside her on a small cot. He felt off balance, as the floor slanted down into the mountain. Her eyes didn't leave him.

"You're his kin," she said knowingly. "The restless one. You look like him. My momma told me what you would look like."

"What can you tell me about him and the treasure?" Connor asked.

She ignored him.

"They say he never found it. Did he?" she asked.

"Not that I know of," said Connor.

"He was not meant to find it. His motives were not pure. You are meant to find it."

Connor was taken aback.

"Why me?" he asked.

"You have a true heart," she answered. "It is wounded and not prideful. It was good to finally meet you," she muttered and drifted back off to sleep.

Connor started to try to speak to her again, to wake her to get the information he was seeking, but the old man grabbed his arm and started to lead him away.

"I guess this was a wild-goose chase," he said under his breath.

He was pulled from the room.

He started to fish for his keys as he was led out the front door.

"A name is not just a name!" he heard her shouting from her room in her frail voice.

He ran back inside and burst back in to find her eyes burning as bright as the sun and staring at him as if in a spell.

"A name is not just a name!" she said again, more softly this time.

She glared at him for a brief period but was not really looking at him. Then she drifted back off to sleep.

Connor left the cottage and began to drive back down the mountain.

He sat on the bench at the roadside drinking hole. He was obviously the only non-native there. *They are friendly enough*, he thought. He sipped his Carib beer that by some miracle of nature was cold. The sun was making its way towards the horizon as the day wound down. He had been here a while, stopping on the way back down the mountain several hours ago. Reggae was wailing softly in the background.

He loved the Caribbean. It was in his blood, Nevis in particular.

The revelation about Kate was still really bothering him, and he didn't know what to do.

A few minutes earlier, the owner of the establishment had given him a cigar. The flavors were nice as he tasted the regionally grown tobacco. He pondered his meeting with Alma. It was hard to make sense of it. Perhaps he was not meant to make sense of it. Maybe things would just happen. *A name is not just a name.*

So what's the next move now? he pondered.

The sun started to cast shadows across the flats at the base of the mountain where he sat. The effect was striking coming off the gravestones in the cemetery across the street from the roadside bar. The shadows created a checkerboard pattern that began to make its way across the road as the sun set.

"You have got to be kidding me!" Connor said aloud as the realization hit him. The old lady's words rang in his ears. *A name is not just a name!*

He knew where to look for the gold.

CHAPTER TWELVE

He made his way in the evening back to Oliver's house on the side of the volcano. The monkeys were chattering up a storm as he walked the short distance from the parked car to the main structure. The shock of Kate's deception had given way to a giddy excitement. She was waiting for him, a melancholy air about her.

"I'm sorry, Connor," she said genuinely as he walked through the door.

"I know where to find the treasure," he said determinedly, the emotion gone from his face.

"I said I'm sorry!"

Kate didn't want to talk about treasure. There was a gnawing pain inside her. She knew she had deceived and hurt him; she wanted everything to be okay.

Kate walked up to him and put her arms around him. He stiffened. "Please forgive me. Don't push me away. In spite of what my job is, I've fallen in love with you."

Connor did nothing for a while. Then he relaxed and slowly put his arms around her waist as well. He felt the small of her back; he smelled her hair. She felt wonderful.

"You are forgiven. I love you too," he said quietly.

They held each other for what seemed an eternity.

After a while, he pulled away. The determined look was back in his face.

"I've got to get back to New York, as soon as possible."

"Okay," she responded. "I guess you will tell me what is going on as soon as you are ready."

"Yes, Agent Kate. When I am ready. And only then," he said.

Two days later, Connor sat in his office in Manhattan. He looked out over the trading floor. The phones were ringing; customers were transacting. The traders were engrossed in their work. Some were seated but many were standing, their arms waving wildly in the air as they yelled into their headsets and fought to find the other side of the trade.

We're making money, he thought. Now it's time to go see if I am right.

After telling his assistant he would be in meetings for the next few hours, he grabbed his sport coat and walked to the exit, then made his way to the nearest subway station one block down the street. He could have taken a cab, but the traffic in the city was notoriously bad, and he had to go all the way downtown. The subway was the fastest and easiest way to get to his destination. Connor bounded down the stairs to the subterranean cavern, swiped his entry card, and caught the downtown express train as the doors closed immediately behind him.

* * *

Miami

Hywel Saunders walked off the jetway in Miami as his flight arrived from Nassau and pushed his way through the crowd milling about the opening of the gate. He was not even nice about it.

How annoying, he thought. To stop at the opening to the gate with hundreds of people behind you and be oblivious to the frustration you're causing other passengers. Amazing. God, it's nice to be intelligent.

He finally cleared the mass of humanity and turned right down the concourse, walking at a brisk clip. The Miami airport was as crowded and inefficient as usual. He hated crowds and craved to be in a less low-class environment. The Miami airport was not the place to be if one disliked crowds. His kind of people didn't deserve to have to deal with all of this riffraff, in his opinion. He longed for some peace and quiet after the short flight.

"Soon, soon," Hywel said to himself. He saw the entrance a quarter mile down on the left.

The Admiral's Club for American Airlines was an easy place to meet and very discreet. He was proud of himself for suggesting this location, but of course he was always proud of himself.

Hywel had been the trustee of the Burr trust for two decades now since Clara had died, and considered himself an expert on all of the intricacies of the situation. It was he who had turned over the trustee duties to Connor Murray. It had been interesting to watch Connor's reaction to reading the documents, and it had not been too difficult to report back on his activities.

That is why I was approached by the client, he thought smugly. They know where to go to get results. He was an arrogant man. Must be the English in me, he mused.

He entered the club and walked upstairs to the main floor after signing in. The room was reserved and catered appropriately as he had requested. His guest would not arrive for thirty minutes.

Now he had some peace and quiet.

He helped himself to a glass of wine. It was useful to calm his nerves and set the mood for the meeting. They should be quite happy with him. He had done their bidding well.

Ever since filing the paperwork with the government assigning the trusteeship for the Burr trust to Connor Murray, Hywel had been busy.

His client had been in touch with him several years before, asking for information about the trust. He knew much more about the situation than Hywel could ever believe. Hywel should have asked some questions and done more due diligence on the client, but then he might have pushed himself away from this opportunity. He thought about it while he sat alone in the conference room.

How did he acquire that amount of data that only the trustee should have been privy to? But he had not wanted to rock the boat. He had smelled opportunity.

Hywel never felt guilty about selling the secrets of the trust. He had built a nice bank account in the Cayman Islands and was able to send both his children to boarding school in England. That had gotten his psychopathic wife off his case and allowed him to have some peace in his life. It was the best decision he had ever made. He had no regrets. Now he had even more information to pass along to his client on the activities of Mr. Murray and the affairs of the trust.

He stood up smartly as the client walked through the door of the conference room. Hywel bowed and then offered the client a glass of wine.

* * *

New York City

Connor hung on to the steel pole that ran from the floor to the ceiling of the not-very-clean subway car. The ride was abrupt and bumpy, much worse than he remembered in the past. He had to hold on tight not to get thrown into the woman standing next to him.

The maintenance on the subway trains had been severely neglected for years now due to budget constraints. It was all over the news. This made for a scary ride sometimes. Recently another woman had been killed by a steel beam falling from the subway tunnel and crashing into one of the cars. He looked nervously at the ceiling.

If it's your time, it's your time, he thought.

He was happy there were no panhandlers on the train today. He had seen the same guy for weeks now getting handouts from tourists with the same old, tired story about needing a ride to Connecticut. The guys selling candy to a captive audience were also annoying. He was always relieved when the doors closed and no one started asking for money from the riders who couldn't move or get away from the beggars. He put that out of his mind and focused on the task in front of him. He could feel the train begin to slow as it approached the next station.

The brakes squealed, and he wondered how the metal kept up with the friction without ruining the entire system. The train began to grind to a halt. He saw the white tile of the subway station come into view, grimy with layers of soot and grease.

Why don't they ever clean those things? he thought. It would not be that difficult and would be much nicer. The thought left his mind as quickly as it had come in.

His mind grew alert. He was almost there—Wall Street station. He had been riding the subway for almost forty minutes.

The train stopped and the doors popped open. People poured out of the car into the people who would not wait and were pushing their way onto the train. *The masses never learn*, he thought. He made his way through the throng, through the turnstyle, and up the stairs into the city above. The noise was deafening. Sirens, horns, and smells greeted him like a lashing to his face. Even the Wall Street protesters were here. *It must be my lucky day. Gotta love New York.*

He walked across the street to Trinity Church and bounced up the stairs and opened the door. It was midmorning so the sanctuary was open.

Immediately an older woman stepped in front of him and put her finger to her lips.

"Shhhh," she said in a self-righteous tone. "We have a baptism going on." Sure enough Connor could see the family and the minister at the head of the church in the dimly lit sanctuary. A small child dressed in white was the center of their attention. Several tourists were also silently viewing the ceremony. He stepped sideways and stood with his hands crossed to take in the view.

The sanctuary was mostly empty except for the people standing. He was struck by how new the structure was. *Not hundreds of years old for sure*, he thought. Noticing a gift shop off to the side of the gathering space, he quietly walked over. The cashier was lazily reading a book, as no one else was in the store. She didn't notice Connor as he entered.

"Excuse me. Where is Captain Kidd's pew?" he asked. Kidd had donated the pew when he was living in New York prior to leaving on his quest with the *Adventure Galley*. He would never see it again.

"Aahhh," she answered. "We get that question often. This is the third building on this site. It has burned down twice. Unfortunately the pew did not survive. Can I interest you in something else? She highlighted some historical books for sale, but Connor was already out the door and making his way to his next objective.

Connor turned and made his way back out the entrance and walked to the side door of the church foyer, which opened into the courtyard. Beyond this was the cemetery. The path meandered among the gravesites, and he strolled slowly towards the far side of the grounds, marveling at the ages of the tombstones as he walked. Some of the old grave markers were barely readable, broken, and withered with age. However, others were very legible with inscriptions from the late 1600s and onward.

The people buried here formed this country, he thought.

There was a large monument towards the western edge of the graveyard. American flags were stuck into the ground around the structure from the recent July Fourth holiday. Someone important was buried here. Four tall concrete urns decorated the monument, which sported a large white obelisk in the center.

Connor walked around it several times slowly. He was incredulous that here lay the person he was chasing through time, trying to find his secrets. *If only he could talk*, he reflected.

What am I looking for? he wondered.

He walked around the monument again. The grass grew over the edges. People walking on the nearby sidewalk from the cross street stared at him through the wrought iron fence and wondered what he was doing. He ignored them.

He stopped and gazed at the front of the edifice in deep thought and tried to remember her words.

A name is not just a name, she had said.

He read the inscription.

"Alexander Hamilton."

Then he saw it.

* * *

Bahamas
Paradise Island

Alex walked along the concrete walkway leading down from the casino toward the line of yachts moored in the marina in the late evening. They were majestic forms illuminated brightly by the Atlantis lights as well as their own. Some were adorned with neon, which added a special artistic touch, the purple light outlining the forms of the ships in the dark, warm night.

There were at least fifteen of them, many as long as a football field it seemed. Immense wealth was needed to operate such vehicles, but that is what typically came to Atlantis on a regular basis. The gambling beckoned as well as the luxurious, beautiful surroundings.

The women were predictable as well. They typically hunted in packs of twos—models, divorcees, et cetera, all looking for that Mr. Right, Mr. Billionaire Right that is. You could see them hawking their wares at the gaming tables and in the bars off the casino floor. Alex often wondered how successful they were in their quest. *It must work, as they keep coming.*

Alex walked past the gift shops and clubs along the marina and made his way towards the last yacht in the row. The nightlife raged around him. Tourists, locals, and the wealthy all mingled together in one big, loud party.

That was fine with Alex. He was worried about being followed, and the mass of people made that harder. The Bahamian night air warmed him as he strolled. He constantly checked behind him, trying to pick out faces in the crowd. However, all he could see were tourists spending their money. It was a busy night.

He was taking no chances.

Alex was startled by a loud banging noise that arose from the walkway behind him. From behind the row of shops came a large, brightly colored mob. He relaxed when he realized it was the Junkanoo. It was a tourist attraction that was routinely performed for the casino.

The elaborate parade of dancers began to snake its way down the same walkway from the row of shops above. The noise was deafening as the fantastically adorned natives danced joyfully past him towards his destination. Drums and noisemakers beat out the dancing rhythm.

There had to be one hundred of them. He waited until they were halfway past and then blended in with them and the many tourists who had drunk way too much rum. They danced as if there were no tomorrow, similar to a high school band in a parade in the United States but on steroids. There was no way anyone could spot him now, much less follow him.

Legend says that during the slave trade decades earlier, the European owners would allow the slaves three days a year during Christmas to express themselves however they wished, within reason of course. So the captives put together bright, colorful costumes and danced like there was no tomorrow down the street to celebrate. That is how Junkanoo was born. Alex was happy to join in.

He exited the mob when he reached the yacht and hopped on

board the stern platform. A door immediately opened and he was let in, almost pulled in. It quickly closed behind him.

He was led into a large cabin outfitted with sunken, leather-bound sofas arranged in a perfect circle. A round table adorned the center. The circle was manned by several Eastern-looking men. There was an open spot where he was obviously meant to sit. He sat in silence for what seemed like an hour.

Finally one of the men leaned forward and spoke.

"Have you found it?" he asked.

"No," Alex replied.

Their faces tightened.

"Why not?" another man asked.

"We don't even know if this exists!" shouted Alex.

"There is no need to raise your voice," said another.

It was surreal sitting there talking to these gentlemen in this way. He could see out the darkened windows the thousands of people milling about the area outside of Atlantis, but these tourists could obviously not see him; little did they know.

"I have been following what he is doing. He hasn't found it yet. And neither have I."

"There is a woman involved," one of the men stated.

"Yes," said Alex. "I do not know who she is but it is very coincidental. I don't like it."

"We know who she is," said the initial speaker. "She is an agent of the United States government. Your fears are confirmed."

Alex's eyes widened. "She has made her way close to him," said Alex. "She will figure it out."

"Then we will take her when the time is right," said the leader.

"When do I get paid?"

"When you produce!" replied the leader.

"When you approached me, I said I would try my best to find what you are looking for. You know I have searched over thirty sites and have betrayed my best friend. I want my money."

"You will have half wired tomorrow. When you produce, the rest will follow."

"Fair enough," said Alex, and he got up to leave.

He was about to exit the door to the cabin and enter the outside world when he turned and said, "I will inform you via the usual way when I find out anything."

Then he opened the door and left the cabin. He blended in nicely with the throng of drunken tourists milling about the esplanade.

* * *

Strait of Hormuz
Persian Gulf
July 10, 2018

Commander Zarin was pleased. He personally had checked every detail and gone over every piece of equipment on his boat. Everything was ready. His crew was trained. This was his moment. He was overcome with joy.

He strolled down the gangplank next to the vessel, rubbing her smooth sides with his hand as he walked. She was his baby. He talked softly to her, caressing her, making her feel his love.

A Chinese-made C-14 Cat-class catamaran missile boat, she was double hulled and sleek. She was also very fast, with a top speed of over fifty knots.

He had made some very specific modifications to meet his requirements. She was originally designed to carry multiple C-701 surface-to-surface missiles, similar to the American Maverick air-to-surface weapon. However, due to their small payload, Commander Zarin had removed all of these and their associated equipment. His boat now carried only one Chinese-made HY-4 surface-to-ship guided missile, an upgraded variant of the well-known Silkworm. This version, in contrast to the original design, had a turbofan engine instead of a liquid-rocket-fueled motor. This weapon also had a much bigger warhead and could sink a large ship, like an aircraft carrier. Once launched, it skimmed over the waves at supersonic speeds and was very difficult to detect and defeat.

But it was a one-shot, one-kill vehicle. He had to be accurate and probably a little bit lucky. And he didn't expect to return, so he didn't require any defensive armaments. They were all removed long ago.

The boat was hidden inside a salt mine at the southeastern end of Queshm Island overlooking the mouth of the strait, an appendage of Iran and a mere twenty-two miles from the mainland at the closest point. The island had been an important trading center for centuries, due to its strategic location in the Gulf. It was a thin, long landmass paralleling the Strait of Hormuz.

The salt mines produced product that was consumed throughout the region. Iran had been masterfully creative in building this underground mooring inside the mine. A need for a waterway to transport the finished salt product allowed for an escape route for the attack boat. The need for large equipment to facilitate the removal of salt for commerce fit nicely with the development of the hiding place for his craft. With the construction done only at night, away from the prying eyes of the satellites and in conjunction with other valid enterprises, his hiding place had been formed.

He now only waited for his orders to attack. He knelt and prayed that his dreams of glory to Allah and martyrdom would be realized.

* * *

January 25, 1813
New York City

Aaron Burr bent down and put his head on the iron railing overlooking New York harbor and cried. A myriad of ships were in various stages of movement in front of him, but it was no longer any matter to him. The January wind off the water was brutal in the cold temperature, but he did not care.

She was gone. He knew it in his heart, but he could not quite accept that his daughter was dead, the light of his life gone.

Burr had been waiting weeks for her arrival in New York. She should have been here almost a month ago. He had been pacing this pier since the New Year. Initially he had been wild with excitement and happiness, as he could not wait to see her, but his heart grew heavier each passing day. He now feared the worst.

She had left Georgetown, South Carolina, on the schooner *Patriot* on New Year's Eve bound to visit her father. The ship was very fast, and they should have arrived a couple of days later. The schooner was previously commissioned as a privateer for the United States against the British in the War of 1812. The guns had been removed and the name changed, but she was still a very capable vessel. The captain, it was thought, wanted to get to New York in a hurry to sell his booty plundered from English ships. The *Patriot* was probably overloaded.

No one had seen or heard from them since.

Many theories over the years emerged as to her fate. The most logical explanation was that the schooner was shipwrecked or attacked by pirates. Another possibility was that she was lured to the North Carolina coast by the "Breakers," a group of criminals who would hang lights around an animal's neck and walk the beach in bad weather. Ship captains would mistake the moving lights for an anchored ship. The unsuspecting crew would draw close seeking shelter and be murdered for the ship's goods.

This was the final straw for Burr. Tragedy had been a constant companion in his life, but this was too much to bear. *Not Theodosia, not Theodosia*, he cried. His body began to heave with convulsions as he wept. In Burr's mind, all was lost.

A strong gust of wind chilled him to his core. His tears froze on the iron railing.

CHAPTER THIRTEEN

New York City

Connor was lost in thought as he walked down 47th Street. It was hot and he was sweating, even at this early hour in the morning. The back of his nicely starched shirt was drenched. The streets of New York were alive around him, but he didn't notice.

His whole world was turned upside down again. Who should he trust? Kate was not who he thought she was. Was her love real or just a pretense to get information? He was confused.

Alex was behaving strangely. That fact disturbed him even more. He had known and trusted Alex for years. Connor's world was unraveling. Everything was becoming gray.

He needed to find some peace and clarity. The trading floor usually provided that. He found purpose in the work, and there was no gray area when it came to making money.

He rounded the corner to his building and entered the turnstile door accessing the lobby. The air conditioning was a welcome relief. Slowly it began to cool the sweat he had worked up during his walk.

Streams of people ahead and behind him were attacking their day in New York City at six forty-five in the morning. *Amazing*, he thought. *If any socialist could see this now, they would realize why capitalism will triumph; these people dressed to the nines determined to make their way in the world this early in the morning. A beautiful thing!*

L TODD WOOD

He reached the elevator still in his own world; however, the people inside were buzzing. Something was happening. He was tired, as he had been entertaining a client late into the previous evening, but he heard bits and pieces of things like "bond vigilantes" and "banana republic." He was jerked out of his stupor and started to pay attention. After all, he was the boss. The small news screen on the elevator was silently flashing some important news, but he didn't get time to read it, as his eyes weren't focusing very well this early in the morning. He needed coffee in a bad way. The lift reached his floor.

The elevator doors opened. He exited and brought out his electronic pass to enter the trading floor; the door beeped and he was allowed access. He passed the receptionist desk and opened the double doors that served as the entrance. An area the size of a football field, the space was filled with lines of trading terminals and hundreds of people. The noise hit him like a ton of bricks.

He required his traders to be on the floor at 7:00 a.m., and at this time people were usually still straggling in. Not today. The floor was in absolute pandemonium.

"What do you mean you don't have a bid for a U.S. Treasury?" screamed one trader incredulously into the phone as Connor walked by on the way to his office on the side of the floor. "You've got to be fucking kidding me!" the trader shouted.

"Oh my God," said Connor to himself. "It's happening."

He reached his office, and thankfully his sales manager was waiting there for him and closed the door behind him.

"Do you know what's going on?" the man asked.

"No," said Connor. "Tell me." He was remiss in not getting up early as usual and reviewing world events, but the dinner the night before had been a long one, and he had chosen to get some rest.

"The Chinese announced last night that they will not be bidding any U.S. Treasuries in the auctions to come this week or in the future, for that matter—at any price."

"Holy shit!" said Connor, shaking his head in disbelief.

"The ten-year just hit eight percent."

"Lord help us. Okay, we have to find a way to make money in this situation and not get killed. I want a meeting of all personnel on the floor in fifteen minutes. Get me our rates analyst in here now!"

Connor was angry; he had seen this coming. Everyone had seen this coming, but there was a denial of reality in Washington. There had been for a long time.

Now there was no more denying anything. No, the shit had hit the proverbial fan; the United States would have to pay the consequences.

The demure forty-year-old woman stepped into Connor's office. She was shell-shocked.

"Well I knew this was coming, but now that it's happening, it's shocking," she said as she took the seat in front of Connor's desk. "I didn't see it happening so quickly!"

"It doesn't matter now," Connor responded. "What matters now for me is that we save this firm in the face of this disaster and add value to our clients. Now what is your view?"

"I think this is an overreaction. The United States will never default on its debts. We should tell clients to buy. The new administration has shown real resolve in dealing with the spending problems."

"Okay then I support you—put that call out to the floor!" Connor instructed. "Now!"

The problem was that China was the biggest buyer of United States Treasury bonds. They owned over $10 trillion of United States debt at this point. Overnight they had told the world that they would no longer be a buyer in U.S. Treasury auctions, which meant the United States had lost its biggest buyer of debt. Now the U.S. would have to offer a much higher interest rate on its new debt to attract buyers in the global market. The question was that no one knew if the United States could pay these new, much higher rates. United

States Treasury bonds were sinking in price like a lead balloon. It was like trying to catch the proverbial falling knife.

Of course we can't service this debt! thought Connor. We have got to get it under control, or we are ruined.

But today he could only save his firm, not his country. Volatility provided an opportunity to do this. Clients would remember who made the right call in this panic. He picked up the phone to call some of their best institutional customers.

* * *

Nassau, Bahamas

Alex reached his car in the parking lot across the street from the Atlantis complex after a five-minute walk from the marina. The lot was relatively empty at this time of night. The nightlife had started to die down. His only company was the occasional drunk couple staggering back to their hotel room from the casino. With privacy assured, he pulled his phone from his pocket and dialed.

"Connor," he spoke as the line answered. His friend sounded frazzled. "You need to come back down as soon as possible. I think I've found another site to explore that has promise." He put on his best face on the phone. It took a few minutes before he could get Connor's full attention.

"Alex, it's going to be a few days. I'm in the middle of a major crisis here, if you haven't heard. Plus they all have been empty, mate."

"Yes, I know they have all been empty, but I have a feeling about this one. Come down at once and bring Kate with you. I'll meet you at the boat in two days in the afternoon. *Ciao.*"

Alex hung up. He hated betraying a friend.

* * *

Kate was still in the Bahamas. She had returned to the institute on Eleuthera. Although she kept up the routines of her cover as best she could, there were too many moving parts to this story for her to do so with precision. She was starting to get questions from the rest of the staff on her comings and goings.

Well I only need to keep it going for a while. Let them wonder, she thought.

One thing was for sure, she was in love with Connor. That had complicated things. She could possibly be fired for allowing this, but so far the situation had not been discovered by her superiors. Fraternization with a person of interest was strictly prohibited.

She had uncovered many suspects in this investigation but kept most of this information from Connor. She was starting to feel bad about this deception.

Hence the rule about fraternizing with the subjects of an investigation, she thought. "What a predicament you have got yourself in now, Kate," she said aloud.

Her current thoughts, however, centered not on Connor but on Alex. She knew Connor trusted him, but she didn't.

She had been betrayed before in this life and could smell a rat. Her father had left her mother when she was a small child, and she missed him terribly. Her mother had never recovered, and probably neither had she.

For her part, Kate never forgot the horror of that feeling of abandonment. There had since been a string of unstable relationships in her life. She was an expert at discerning the true intentions of people, the result of living betrayal firsthand. Her senses were fine-tuned. She had spent her life attempting to glean people's true motives. Her experience as a child had taught her that. Perhaps she questioned too much sometimes, but with Alex she had no doubt there was more there than met the eye. She just didn't know the whole story yet.

Kate didn't want Connor hurt. Therefore she had been looking into Alex on many levels.

The results were not pretty. He obviously led multiple lives. Drug running, money laundering, and other serious crimes were suspected of him but had never been proved. He was another person of interest in her current investigation.

He's a bad guy, she thought. And Connor has no idea.

She read through more communications from her intelligence group regarding the alliance and the findings on Alex.

"I'm going to have to protect him and not allow my feelings for him to interfere. This is going to be a tough balancing act to walk," she said aloud.

Kate could tell Russian involvement when she saw it. It was the raw brutality that always struck her. The Machiavellian tactics were usually unmistakable. It was the centuries of dictatorships and a history of a cruel life. Suffering was a Russian pastime. It was an art form. The past continued to influence their behavior and probably always would.

The centuries of experience with authoritarian regimes and Russian respect of raw power had created their way of conducting business. There was a unique sadness to Russian society. A sense of expectations of greatness forever wasted and tied to the boot on the throat. They were forever practicing the art of war. She wondered what could ever change the Russian status quo.

It was the way they treated the girls. Of course they were young and beautiful, stunningly so. However, you could sense the fear lurking behind their eyes. The way they were just sitting quietly and waiting for instructions from their companions, not even talking to each other. It was sad. She had seen it all before. In many ways, the feminist revolution had not made its way to Eastern Europe. Sometimes she wondered if that was a good or a bad thing, but what she was seeing was bad.

Kate took a break from looking through her binoculars at Alex sitting on the deck of the Cricket Club down below. Her eyes were tired. She was mingling with the tourists on the walls of Fort Charlotte. The view overlooked the harbor and the buildings below her, perched as they were on the sloping land towards the fort.

She knew Alex would be there drinking at this time. It was like clockwork. He was Russian. So she had decided to take a chance and do some surveillance. Her luck had been good. He showed around five and drank by himself for a while. He occasionally would have a flirting discussion with one of the native waitresses. However, she could tell he was anxious. He was waiting for someone.

Expectedly, an hour later four table guests showed up, two older, hard-looking men and two beautiful young women on their arms. The men were engaged in serious talk now for some time while the girls just sat there looking pretty.

Kate could tell they were Russian, as she had lived in Moscow for three years following graduate school, where she had earned a degree in international relations with a focus on Russia. She had been hired by a clandestine branch of the U.S. government focusing on combating international financial threats to the United States. She had learned a great deal during her time there. In fact, she had cut her teeth on the business there. Her experience would come in handy, and she now relied on those honed instincts.

She had now seen enough. The sun would be down soon, and her visibility would be gone. She knew what she had to do. She had to go to Moscow. She walked casually back to her vehicle with a throng of British sightseers and disappeared into the crowd.

* * *

They sat on the stern drinking wine as the sun set over the ocean, creating a fiery scene. The boat rocked slowly as the waves lapped against the sides gingerly, occasionally splashing up the side over the rail. The sound was soothing, and Kate wished she could just be alone here on this boat for a week with Connor. But that was not to be; it was not reality.

Kate wondered if this was where the Caribbean people had picked up their patented pastel hues, as the pinks and yellows blasted the heavens off the setting sun. The colors were spectacular. A warm breeze bathed them from across the waves.

They had spent the day since arriving back in Nassau driving the *Soulmishka*, Alex's boat, out to the Exuma Cays again, searching for the spot that Alex had found. They had anchored off the cay towards dusk and decided to wait to dive in the morning. Connor felt naked here without his phone but had access to the internet from the equipment on Alex's boat. He wasn't totally cut off. In a few minutes he could be in touch with the desk in New York if need be. He was happy he hadn't been interrupted so far. He had missed Kate, more than he'd expected. It felt right to be with her.

Alex seemed to be in a better mood than usual. He had surprised them with several bottles of very expensive wine and other goodies.

They dined on cheese, crackers, fruit, and sausages until the sun set. They enjoyed the evening together. Kate was her usual jolly self in spite of her fears about Alex. They ate and drank into the wee hours of the morning.

Eventually she and Connor retired to the cabin while Alex slept on a cot on the stern in the open air. The waves sloshed against the hull, and they all, one by one, drifted off to sleep.

He was there again. Looking out across the seemingly small distance and staring at her in the window of the other tower. It seemed as though he could reach out and touch her face, but the length to the other tower was just too great. He couldn't quite remember what she looked like; the face was blurry. It had been so long.

She was pleading at him with her eyes. He could sense her fear and horror.

"Please, Connor! Help me! Help our son!"

Connor looked beside her and saw the small boy holding his mother's hand. A boy he would never meet.

"Please, Daddy! It hurts!" the boy cried.

Then the fire crept into the office where they were standing. They started to burn.

She looked at Connor one last time, grabbed her boy's hand tighter, and they both jumped into the abyss.

Connor awoke violently, emptying his lungs in pain. Kate had to struggle to hold him as he thrashed in bed.

"Connor!" she screamed. "Stop! You're with me!"

He slowly got his bearings and calmed down.

A few minutes later he began to speak. His body was shaking.

"I received the lab results a week later in the mail. She had been to the doctor for routine tests. There was a message on the machine asking her to call the doctor's office. She was pregnant, for God's sake! I had a son!"

His voice started to break.

"I think she knew and was waiting to tell me. I found baby clothes in the closet."

He broke down.

"It's haunting me," he finally said.

"Connor," she said after holding him for a while, stroking his hair. "I had a dream last night too. It was Emily. She asked me to take care of you and to tell you she loves you and your son loves you. I love you too."

Connor pulled her close and kissed her softly. He rolled on top of her and entered her forcefully, so much that she screamed. They made love violently. Connor released all of the hurt, frustration, and pain that had been building up for years. They melted together.

The nightmares ceased.

They drifted off again to sleep.

Later in the blackness, he awoke with her naked body next to him spooned closely. She was still wet from their lovemaking. He entered her again from behind. She was still asleep but welcomed him. He was very hard and she pulsated around him as he again took her. They fell asleep again together.

* * *

Nassau, Bahamas

The Chinese man sat in the conference room at the far head of the table. Coffee and several varieties of tea adorned the credenza against the window, along with bottled water and other drinks. A dirty hot plate sat discarded against the window. There was no one else in the room.

He was not accustomed to being kept waiting, and he had been waiting for fifteen minutes.

The carpet was stained, and the table and chairs were old, but there was an attempt at formality and pomp and circumstance in the room. The Formica was chipped off the table, and books were strewn around the back of the space. Several of the chairs around the table were broken, and wobbled when sat on.

The man wasn't impressed but he continued to wait.

A few minutes later there was movement from a door almost hidden in the wallpaper across from where the man was sitting. He stood up as the prime minister of the Bahamas and an aide walked into the room.

The prime minister walked briskly around the table with his hand extended in friendship.

"Mr. Lu, the people of the Bahamas are most grateful for the loan of three hundred million U.S. dollars. We will make good use of the money to develop our infrastructure for the next hundred years." He shook his guest's hand firmly and then walked to the head of the long conference table and sat. Out of formality, the guest sat as well, subconsciously hoping the chair did not collapse beneath him.

There was a brief silence, and then the guest spoke.

"Mr. Prime Minister, the People's Republic of China is very happy to assist you in your development. Our people are most generous. We are glad we can share some of our commercial success with others. We shall continue to be a friend of the Bahamas."

"Why thank you, Mr. Lu," the prime minister responded in an overly friendly manner.

"We do have one request, however, sir, if you could be so kind?" Mr. Lu asked.

"Of course, sir, do tell!" the prime minister said. He began to fidget in his seat uncomfortably.

"Well sir, we have been privy to information that your office has been siphoning resources from the expeditions we are funding."

The guest leaned forward in his chair toward the leader of the Bahamas. "Please ask your aide to leave," he said quietly.

The prime minister stared for what seemed an eternity. Then he nodded at the junior official, and the younger man got up and left the conference room through the same door in the wallpaper.

"Mr. Prime Minister," the guest said once the man had left. "I don't care if you get rich off of our little endeavor." All the diplomatic pretenses were gone. "However, the mother lode, if found, will be given to us! Do you understand?"

"I think we have an understanding," the prime minister responded curtly.

"Good, then I will trouble you no further."

The guest then shook his hand, bowed, and left the room.

CHAPTER FOURTEEN

Summer 2018
Iran, Persian Gulf

The shipments now became routine. The Bushehr nuclear plant was completed years ago, with Russian help of course. The construction was hailed as an achievement in Iranian peaceful intentions and Russian diplomacy. The plant was being built only for energy generation, according to both parties, and was proof that the world was wrong concerning Iran. It was operated by Russian specialists and the spent fuel said to be sent back to Russia, although Iran was scheduled to take over control of the plant within a few years.

The agenda behind the Iranian nuclear program was peaceful— this was the story both countries wanted the world to swallow. Russia had started construction of other nuclear plants in Iran as well and was providing nuclear technology and assistance in a variety of ways. Russia considered a nuclear Iran an American problem, and stopping the program was not in their national interests.

Bushehr was started by the Shah in the 1970s by German contractors. It was hailed as the first peaceful nuclear electrical plant in the Middle East. After the Iranian Revolution, progress was halted, as the initial contractors pulled out. Progress was further delayed, as the partially completed project was damaged by air strikes during the Iran-Iraq War. The Russians resumed construction in the mid-1990s, and after many delays, the plant became operational in late 2011. It supplied two percent of the country's electrical needs.

The large trucks thundered across the terminal at the nearby port in the dark of night after loading their cargo from the container ship. There were four of them. The drive to the power plant had been uneventful. Soon they entered the covered storage area inside the protected walls of the complex. Therefore, the view was blocked from the American satellites orbiting overhead. They came to a halt inside the structure. Immediately, activity sprang up around them as cranes appeared overhead and the covers were removed from the shipments. Senior Iranian military officials looked on from the floor above with satisfaction on their faces.

The trucks did not contain peaceful nuclear construction materials. The cargo was much more immediately lethal to the West. The main concern of Western intelligence was the delivery of nuclear materials that could be used for production of a weapon. Although the Iranians were well advanced in this effort, this was not the cargo this evening.

The trucks contained Russian-made S-300 surface-to-air-missiles, or SAMs. These were one of the most feared weapon systems in the world. Initially deployed in the late 1970s, the weapon was battle tested and reliable. The system was upgraded and its accuracy and effectiveness improved over and over again. The elegant simplicity of Russian weapon systems allowed this. It could track up to one hundred targets and engage more than ten at a time. These targets included cruise missiles, aircraft, and even ballistic missiles. In the hands of the Iranians, they would provide a powerful capability and deterrent to Western attacks on their nuclear program, hence the installation of the systems at the nuclear plant and other sensitive sites around Iran.

These missiles were a deadly menace to Western Air Force assets.

For decades the Soviets and now the Russians had developed powerful weapons to counter the perceived Western edge in air superiority. He who rules the sky rules the battlefield, as Billy Mitchell, the father of the American Air Force, foreshadowed. The Russians were brilliant in developing uncomplicated but powerful systems to engage Western aircraft and to protect their ground assets. Their air defense networks were in high demand globally.

The most potent among them was the late-model long-range S-300. They were coveted by the Iranians.

For their part, the Russians publicly denied Iran access to this very sophisticated system several years back in a bid to the Americans and their push for sanctions against Iran at the U.N. But the ban was not to last, if it was ever really serious.

The West was terrified of a nuclear-armed Iran. Iran had claimed over and over again publicly that it wanted to "wipe Israel off the map."

The Russians, in preventing access to these missiles, gained from the perception that they were cooperating with the U.N. They also gained some flexibility with the current U.S. administration, which helped Moscow with reciprocation on some of Russia's pet projects as well. Turning a blind eye to the continued conflict in Chechnya and the removal of American missile defense systems in Europe were two examples.

The Russian action was just temporary and not meant to last. It was a ruse. Russia craved the respect and financial reward it received from expanding its armament export empire, and there was no love lost between the Russian leadership and the Americans. It was a simple lie.

The missiles were unloaded from the trucks and stored safely out of view of the world.

* * *

Bahamas

Connor awoke to the sound of the waves hitting the side of the boat. It was a peaceful sound, not violent. The seagulls were also cawing overhead. He instantly realized where he was and that he had to get up in an hour to go search another site in the cays with Alex. It was a wild-goose chase, he knew. Whatever had been hidden there was long gone. He realized that now. The boat rocked slowly.

It was still black outside at 5:00 a.m. Kate stirred beside him. He pulled her close and felt her naked body. Carnal thoughts passed through his head, but he decided to let her sleep. He put his arm around her, spooning her. She made a very feminine sound and backed into him.

Is this love? he wondered. *It might be*, he told himself. He had not let his heart feel this emotion in a long time. It excited and also scared him.

He could hear the gulls starting to scream on the land nearby as the sun started to rise. The light would not be long now. He drifted back to sleep with her in his arms.

The light peeked through the cabin window, and Kate awoke first this time. She turned and looked at Connor sleeping peacefully; she was thankful for this.

God knows he needs it, she thought to herself.

She got up and relieved herself in the head and climbed back into the bed next to Connor. This time he awoke and looked at her.

"You're beautiful," he marveled aloud.

"I need to tell you something," she stated firmly.

He became fully awake and looked at her questioningly, sitting up on his elbow.

"It's Alex. He's not who you think he is. He has a past. Ha, and a present for that matter," she corrected herself softly.

"What do you mean?" Connor whispered.

"I've been checking into him. Once you've been betrayed in your life, you develop a sixth sense. He's not clean, Connor."

She sat up and looked him in the eyes, holding the sheet over her body.

She began to speak deliberately.

"We think the Chinese are after the treasure as well, and they might have company. They have been buying gold reserves all over the world, and this would be a freebie. I think that is who was in our house in Nevis. I also think Alex is in bed with them. I don't have direct proof, but I do know that a large sum of money was recently wired into one of Alex's offshore accounts in Cayman. It came from an entity we know is controlled by a Chinese military company."

"Shit," Connor said sadly.

"I think he is using us to find whatever it is that Burr or Hamilton hid."

Connor lay on the bed in disbelief. How could a best friend do this to him? Again, his whole life was being turned upside down.

"Don't take it out on yourself," she said. "He has lived a double life for a long time now that you have known nothing about."

They both sat there in silence listening to the sound of the sea.

"I have to confront him," Connor finally said.

"At the right time," she responded.

* * *

Somewhere in the Caribbean Sea

The yacht moved effortlessly through the three-foot waves. She was a well-designed craft, built for speed and comfort. The large crew took care of every detail and performed like clockwork. The massive interior quarters resembled any Wall Street conference room with ease. No luxurious detail had been spared. The passengers inside barely felt any disturbance from the rolling swells. This was fortunate, as they needed to focus on the task at hand.

They were seated around the sunken table, a round table if you will, so no one would feel less important. The national egos involved here were an issue to be dealt with.

This was deadly serious business. When one is making war against a superpower that is not entirely aware of it, one must be careful and deliberate in one's decisions. Even if that superpower is waning in its capability to project power, one must be sure of one's actions.

"The Americans will never respond. They are too weak," the Russian said first. "We must strike while we have the opportunity." He reached out to accept tea from a steward who was making the rounds while he spoke. He waited for the next person to interject. He didn't like the Chinese or the Iranians, but for now they served a purpose, Russia's longer-term purpose. But he was wary; he didn't trust any of these men.

"I have no problem attacking, but we must be sure the time is right. We are in no hurry. We will not have a second chance at this and must undertake this endeavor correctly," said one of the Chinese participants. "The tiger still has his teeth."

"Our forces are ready," said the Iranian. "We are ready to bring the Great Satan to her knees. We are ready to start this conflict that is demanded by God. He will have us prevail."

"Enough of the religious crap," said the Chinese representative arrogantly. "Our governments have agreed to work together to destroy the United States of America. The Chinese people have done our part to devalue their currency and to control most of the precious metal and rare earth resources in the world. Now your job is to drive them into bankruptcy by starting a war they cannot afford but will surely try to prosecute."

"The Iranian armed forces will do their duty," said the Iranian diplomat. "We are massing as we speak for the attack. Our casualties will be heavy, but our strength and determination will never be broken."

"And the Russian people will begin to sell their U.S. Treasury securities immediately upon the start of hostilities," the Russian emissary added. "We will also stop using the dollar as a trade currency, which will add further downward pressure on its value. The swap lines between the ruble and the yuan have been established."

"As will the Chinese. The American's economic power will be decimated," said the Chinese leader. "The United States dollar will cease to be a global currency. At that time we will gather here again and make plans to destroy her power completely."

* * *

Scientific Institute
Eleuthera, Bahamas

Kate paced the floor in her room at the compound. She had to clear her mind to think.

She loved Connor. He deserved to be loved. But could she always be there for him? Her job could take her anywhere in the world. It was dangerous. What would happen to him if he lost another woman? Well, he was strong; she knew that. But he might never trust and love again. Was it best to break it off now? Before anyone got hurt? She knew in her heart that this investigation could take her down very difficult and dangerous paths. The future of her country was more important to her than a relationship with a lover. She had made this decision on priorities in her life long ago. She had taken an oath. An oath she meant to uphold. Nothing had changed in her mind to make her alter that path.

She paced some more and took another sip of black tea. It helped calm her nerves. She looked out the balcony window at the rolling blue surf pounding the beach. The stillness was captivating. She loved the peacefulness here.

What a beautiful scene, she thought. Too bad I can't enjoy it.

They had searched the cay that Alex had identified as a possible location of the gold. It had of course turned up empty. There had been a surreal feeling the entire time during the dive that Alex's heart was not in the search. That made Kate wonder even more what was happening.

"Alex felt our cautiousness," she said to herself.

Now she was frightened. What was going on? She drank more tea. It was going to be a rough night.

She considered pulling out her ace in the hole.

"It is not time yet for that," she said aloud.

To say that Kate was connected was an understatement.

During her college years at Haverford in Pennsylvania, she became fast friends with a certain Elizabeth Walker. After rooming together the first semester as freshmen, they became inseparable. Kate was even the maid of honor at Elizabeth's wedding several years back. They were like sisters from a different mother. In fact, Elizabeth's mother had died of cancer earlier in her childhood. She had been raised by her father, and Kate had become like a second child to him.

It just so happened that Mr. Walker was then governor of Pennsylvania, and had gone on recently to become the president of the United States.

No, it was not time to play that card yet.

Kate knew what she had to do. She had to distance herself from Connor. Her country was facing a mortal threat. She could no longer allow her feelings for him to interfere with her duty to her oath.

Out of college, Kate was recruited by a shadowy government agency. Once on board and through training, she was asked to join a highly selective team tasked with protecting the economic stability of the United States of America. She earned this assignment by her own hard work and talent. She was not going to throw away her reputation by crying to the president for help.

She was close to finding out who the entity was and the agenda behind that threat. Personal feelings could not be allowed to jeopardize this effort. There were people depending on her. The whole damn country was depending on her. She would figure it out on her own and stop them.

She made her decision.

She would get out of Connor's life, however painful that may be to both of them.

***

July 15, 2018
Strait of Hormuz

It was 2:00 a.m. when Commander Zarin and his crew of nine silently left the secluded cover of the salt mine and slowly made their way out of the man-made canal into the open ocean. The sky was overcast, so they relied on night vision goggles for navigation, but even these did not provide much help in the blackness. They were thankful for the low visibility; it would provide concealment. They had eaten their last meal and prayed to Allah for glory. They were ready. They were ready to meet their God.

The U.S. Navy task force was making its way through the Strait of Hormuz a few miles in front of them, protecting the crucial channel and ensuring free navigation of international waters.

The U.S. Fifth Fleet had completed this maneuver hundreds of times over the years in their effort to keep this critical waterway open for international commerce and specifically twenty percent of the world's oil supply. It was a routine mission.

There had been hostilities in the past. The conflict had resulted in the sinking of multiple Iranian naval vessels and the accidental downing of an Iranian airliner by the USS *Vincennes* in the 1980s.

The Iranian Navy during this time had mined the strait in order to impede the flow of oil to the West. A U.S. ship struck one of these mines and was almost sunk. In response, the Americans destroyed several Iranian armed oil platforms and sunk several enemy craft of various sizes.

The airline disaster was the result of an overexcited captain aboard the U.S. ship, who thought the airliner was an Iranian F-14 commencing an attack run. It was unfortunate and highlighted the fog of war that Clausewitz had written about. In war, decisions are sometimes made without all of the critical information.

That was some time ago, and no one was expecting what was about to happen. The American radars and other sensors were active, but there was not a sense of urgency. The Iranians now hoped to exploit this.

Commander Zarin was not the only one silently leaving their harbor. Over three hundred small vessels, which had been painstakingly hidden over the last twelve months, were making their way into the open ocean from their places of concealment. Soon the American radars would pick them up, but it would be too late. At the appropriate prearranged time, under radio silence, all of the small vessels gunned their engines and made their way towards the American force. They swarmed like bees as they rushed the much larger ships.

It was asymmetric warfare at its finest.

* * *

Lieutenant Vince Armstrong was in the officers' mess having coffee with two other off-duty naval officers when the call to battle stations startled him and the others. He gulped the half-full mug down and slammed it on the table, racing to the flight deck of the USS *Nashville*, which was his post. The ship was an amphibious assault vessel full of U.S. Marines, their vehicles, and gear. Their assigned mission was to deploy U.S. Marines anywhere in the world to project American power. There was a helipad on the rear of the ship for rotary wing landings.

He arrived on the flight deck a minute later and donned his battle gear. The flight control area was submerged beneath the deck, with only a glass encasement rising from the ship to allow the controllers to put their heads above the deck to direct flight operations.

Once inside, he asked the on-duty officer for a status report to get up to speed on the situation at hand.

"We have a CH-53 inbound," said the duty officer. "He's bringing supplies. Thirty seconds out."

"We'll he'd better hurry," said Lt. Armstrong.

He grabbed the microphone for the air control frequency.

"Specter Two-Six, this is Alpha One. Proceed with haste. Situation on board," he ordered.

Below decks, the company of U.S. Marines on board were also stowing their gear and preparing for the worst. It was like being a passenger on an airplane. There was absolutely nothing they could do during a naval engagement but wait there in the hull like the sitting ducks they were. They waited for the day when they could be deployed in-country or storm a beach, as they had been trained. Here they were useless.

They donned battle gear, checked and tightened the tie-downs on their vehicles, and waited.

* * *

Commander Zarin raced into the open water. He was thrilled and consumed with passion for his God. Soon he would go to him. His emotions were overwhelming.

He could not see or hear them, but he knew that hundreds of other boats were massing on the same targets, the elements of the U.S. Fifth Fleet currently steaming through the strait.

He barked commands to his crew.

"Turn on the radar and prepare to fire!" he said loudly but calmly.

He was at peace and ready to meet his maker.

* * *

In the electronic control room of the USS *San Jacinto*, the radar emissions of Commander Zarin's craft were noted by the electronic warfare officer, who relayed countermeasures and notified his commander. But it was one of many signatures painted on the scope. There were hundreds of targets, and they were busy trying to prioritize and engage each one. The *San Jacinto* was the Aegis-class ship responsible for defending the fleet against attack. Its advanced radar tracking system could engage over a hundred targets at once.

But tonight even this system was not up to the task at hand.

The commander of the task force had already given the order to fire in order to defend his force. The electronic warfare officer passed this target to a U.S. Air Force asset circling above. *This is obviously the real thing*, the lieutenant junior grade thought. The adrenaline rushed through his veins.

* * *

Commander Zarin fired the Silkworm missile at the nearest target that displayed on his radar. The missile roared from the catamaran and screamed towards the ship. Simultaneously he saw fireballs emerge up and down the strait to his left and right as other Iranian ships fired as well. He felt a joy he had never experienced before. He was doing God's will. He closed his eyes and prepared to meet his maker.

* * *

The Marine CH-53 was hovering over the helipad at the stern of the ship. Lt. Armstrong was in communication with the pilot, talking him down in the darkness. This was a delicate operation.

The pilot of the aircraft had no visible horizon as he stared out into the blackness of the night ocean sky. It was literally like looking into a black hole. He could not tell if he was moving up, down, left, or right. The only information he had was that provided by his instruments and his crew.

The ship bobbed up and down beneath him. As he tried to maintain a level hover over the moving ship, his crew talked him down.

"Left one, right two, down one," the flight engineer said as he looked down at the helipad through his night vision goggles. The tubes magnified tiny amounts of ambient light and provided a greenish, fuzzy picture to those wearing them. Even so, the crewman could barely see the deck below him on this dark night. Finally, with only a few feet separating the helicopter from the ship, the pilot pushed down the collective and slammed the aircraft onto the deck. The crewmen raced in to tie her down as the cargo was unloaded. It was more of a controlled crash than a landing.

As the wheels connected with the ship, the copilot looked out the left side of his windscreen into the blackness over the ocean. He saw a bright spot of light heading directly for the ship at supersonic speed. He yanked up on the collective to get the helicopter airborne and screamed into the mic at the same time.

"Missile inbound!" he shouted.

It was too late.

The warhead struck the rear doors of the LPD, obliterating the stern of the vessel. The fireball engulfed the helicopter. Water rushed into the hold of the ship, where the Marines were waiting.

Lt. Armstrong had one final look at the sky before Marine armaments below exploded and blew the ship in half.

CHAPTER FIFTEEN

Kate read the lab report that was displayed on her computer screen but wasn't surprised. She had expected as much.

The shell casing she had picked up off the floor that night in Oliver's home was from a Chinese-made QSZ-92 pistol, the most recent product of Chinese arms factories. It was either a very good plant to lead her in the wrong direction or another piece of circumstantial evidence that lead her down the road to Beijing. The shooter himself she would have called definitely Oriental, and most likely Chinese. She had gotten a good look at him while they were in the bar at the old sugar mill.

This was one piece of evidence.

She had more, much more.

Kate had a Top Secret security clearance. However, she was cleared several layers higher than that on a need-to-know basis for her current position. This was an SCI authorization, or Sensitive Compartmented Information. Per this access, she had available to her the most sensitive data the National Security Agency, or NSA, could collect via their sophisticated electronic eavesdropping capabilities.

As she scanned the data on her secure connection in her hotel room in Nassau, more strands of the conspiracy began to come to light. Before and after the initiation of hostilities in the Persian Gulf, there was a marked increase in intelligence chatter between the Iranian, Chinese, and Russian diplomatic apparatuses. They had caught them red-handed.

Why hadn't anyone else put this information together? The Chinese and the Russians had for years been making overt statements about removing the United States from its position of dominance on the world stage. The Chinese had manipulated their currency to swell their trade imbalance. By keeping their currency value artificially low, they created an artificially low price for Chinese goods in their export markets around the world. This in turn created massive currency reserves, primarily in U.S. dollars.

They also pushed a global mercantilist agenda and bought influence around the world. The recent cash disbursement to the Bahamas was just one example.

Billions of dollars had been loaned or granted to multiple Caribbean nations for infrastructure development. Jamaica, the Bahamas, the Dominican Republic, and Barbados were the main recipients. Sports facilities, refineries, roads, bridges, et cetera had all been funded. Economic growth was anemic in these regions, as they relied primarily on tourism to fund their economies. This had been lacking since the long-term downturn began almost a decade before. The Chinese had stepped in to fill the void.

They also were pushing for access to commodities and raw materials globally. Africa was in the forefront here. In fact, many of the indigenous African people had become wary of Chinese bringing money. They complained of labor abuse and exploitation and strong-arm tactics in negotiations. Raw materials and energy were especially targeted for influence. Farm land, rare earth minerals, petroleum reserves, et cetera were bought and paid for.

The Bahamas was a large benefactor of Chinese largesse. Hundreds of millions in loans were issued and forgiven. The Caribbean was a very strategic area with its plethora of ports near the United States. Now the Chinese were taking action in concert with other world players that wished the United States harm.

The United States was at war with the world. The president needed to know this. It was time. She picked up the secure phone and called the White House.

* * *

The Caribbean

The British Empire literally ruled the world. Or at least they used to. Connor was amazed at how much their presence was still felt throughout the globe. The economic reach they had sustained for centuries was incredible. Australia, the Americas, Africa, India, Hong Kong, and of course the Caribbean all felt the English legacy.

Connor stood on the deck surrounding the pool overlooking Kingston, Jamaica. The hotel was located atop one of the nearby famous Blue Mountains. The view was breathtaking. The sun was setting over the harbor, and the lights of the sprawling city began to twinkle. *It's so beautiful*, he thought.

He had arrived that morning to meet with several clients in Kingston. That part of a trip to Jamaica was always unpleasant. The city was like a war zone. Gang warfare was common, and the streets were very dangerous. Truckloads of armed soldiers were frequently seen driving from place to place. Many times they hit up the taxi drivers for bribes when they saw them with a foreign fare. Trash littered the streets in front of the decaying buildings.

There were pockets of modern living. A few nice hotels existed. The financial buildings were typically professional, as were the businessmen and -women.

It was not a pleasant job to sit in the rear of the hired car and be driven swiftly from place to place. Going from meeting to meeting and being worried about being mugged was not his strong suit.

That was the emerging-market business. It was the same in

Venezuela, Trinidad, and other parts of Latin America. It came with the job.

Connor was always struck by the natural abundance in Jamaica. The bananas, coffee, and tourism were always big revenue producers for the country. In addition, the land itself was one huge piece of bauxite sticking out of the Caribbean Sea. Bauxite was one of the main ingredients of aluminum.

However, the left-of-center governments could never seem to create the right conditions to exploit this advantage. Their cost of production was thirty percent higher than the competition's, so they were unprofitable in the international market.

A shame, thought Connor.

The English influence was unmistakable, however, during his travels. The language was an obvious giveaway. Jamaica, although ruled by the French as well for a time, was built on the English model. The population descended mainly from slaves imported to work the sugar plantations and from their English masters. Throughout the Caribbean, cricket was the national sport, as in the Bahamas. The passion for the game was just as high here.

Many islands in the Caribbean still had the Queen's imprint on their currency. The main connection, however, which Connor saw on a daily basis, was financial. The primary financial centers of the world were English-based: Cayman, London, New York, Hong Kong.

However, he also saw that this was changing. There was a new sheriff in town, the Chinese. Economic power was definitely moving east, where it had been centuries before.

The Chinese, flush with their trillions in foreign currency reserves and holding the economic reins of America with their trillions in U.S. dollar debt, were now spreading their influence throughout the globe.

He was well aware that for years they had been buying access to natural resources across the world. Oil in Latin America, strategic minerals in Africa, and access to ports in the Caribbean were acquired. This was done in full view of several U.S. administrations, who were too busy worrying about making their banker angry to deal with the obvious threats to national security.

Now their chief aim was to supplant the United States dollar with the Chinese yuan as the new global reserve currency. They no longer were so helplessly linked to the U.S. consumer market. Their middle class was growing exponentially. They were creating their own domestic market. The United States had lost its influence.

This was obvious to Connor and to most people in the financial business. There was more and more bond issuance in yuan than in dollars. The Russians and the Chinese were conducting most of their international trade in their own currencies rather than the historical U.S. dollar standard for several years now.

The response of the United States to all of these issues was disheartening. The administration was pursuing a policy of devaluing the currency to deal with their external debt problem. No country had ever successfully followed this course and come out ahead economically.

Many a banana republic had tried—Zimbabwe, Argentina, and others—but the process didn't work. It always led to inflation, loss of economic power, and a lower standard of living for its citizens. A nation can't devalue its way to prosperity.

Connor mused on all of this as he smoked a nice Jamaican cigar. *One of life's small pleasures*, he thought.

The recent hostilities in the Persian Gulf would add even more economic pressure to the United States. They could not afford to prosecute another very expensive war.

We can't borrow the money, he pondered.

Interest rates had already risen dramatically, which greatly increased the cost of servicing all of this debt. The value of the United States currency was plummeting.

America's financial crisis was entering a final stage.

After all, Connor thought, it's what spelled the end for the British Empire. They just could not afford the fight with the Nazis. They could not afford to maintain their empire. It just crumbled. History repeats itself, he mused.

* * *

Kate got off the spanking-brand-new Aeroflot Boeing jet and walked into Moscow's Sheremetyevo airport. It was a sparkling-new facility, built to ease the crowding of the city's older airport, Domodedovo, located across town. The nouveau riche Russian money was very much on display. Packed duty-free shops lined the corridors. The locals were flush with cash. Beautiful girls dressed to the nines were everywhere.

Wow, how much has changed in the last decade, she said to herself as she remembered her time here years ago. Then, there had been a palpable sense of doom in the air, but no longer. The one thing the government had provided was economic success, at least in the cities. People did not have political freedom, but they very much had opportunity, to a certain degree. That is, *if* they knew the right people.

She made her way to passport control. It was always a tense moment, she recalled. The harsh looks and the stare-down were standard. It was an automatic Russian response to foreigners, especially Americans. She wondered if her cover was blown and she would be targeted for surveillance, or even if she would be let in the country.

She seemed to pass through immigration easily enough. *Who knows?* she thought.

She waited forever at baggage claim. I have traveled to many airports in many different countries, and the luggage always is late, she said to herself. She waited for an eternity.

I knew I shouldn't have checked my bag.

Finally the baggage arrived, and she poured herself into a taxi and barked in Russian for the driver to take her to the Moscow Hilton.

Kate was fluent. She had studied the language all through college and then immersed herself in the culture when she lived in Moscow. Although it had been a while, it came back naturally and easily. She rather enjoyed speaking it again.

The drive to the hotel was uneventful. What struck her was the continuity of Moscow. Yes, the signs on the shops were more vibrant. The cars on the road were nicer and much more expensive. But the buildings were for the most part the same Stalinist Soviet-designed housing blocks that had existed for decades. In spite of a new section of the city sporting new skyscrapers, it was as if the Russians could not escape the past. That thought was even more pungent as she thought of what was going on with the conflicts globally. The Russian Machiavellian instinct again showed itself.

She could not help but think that if there had been a more concerted effort at democracy after the fall of the Soviet Union, maybe things would have turned out differently. However, the complexes of the Russian leadership had prevented that. She hardly thought the Russian people were anti-American. "You are just like us!" many of them had told her. She could hear the surprise in their voices, once they had gotten to know her. They were, however, routinely whipped into an anti-American fervor by the frequent government television shows that demonized America. If one listened to this propaganda, one would think the United States was behind every sneaky plot ever imagined and then some.

Kate firmly believed in engaging people of different cultures. *The more you get to know each other, the harder it is to hate each other*, she thought.

She arrived at the hotel.

The Moscow Hilton was housed in one of seven towers that Stalin had built in the early twentieth century to ostensibly highlight Soviet prowess in architecture. The real truth was that Stalin feared being ridiculed by Westerners upon their arrival in Moscow. "You have no skyscrapers!" he could hear them say. So Stalin demanded Moscow grow its skyline.

Complexes again, she thought.

Eight were designed but only seven were built. Chronically overengineered, they were too heavy, and many of the floors were unusable. However, they were beautiful. "The Seven Sisters," Westerners called them.

The tower encompassing the hotel was one of the smaller structures. The other larger sister buildings boasted Moscow University, government buildings, and other hotels. The university today was still the tallest building used solely for education in the world.

The Moscow Hilton had reopened several years ago after an extensive renovation. The floors were lined with exquisite marble. The ceilings were adorned with ornate carvings and art. It was quite remarkable.

After checking in and refreshing herself in her room, she had a drink in the lounge in the lobby of the hotel. She wanted to reorient herself with Russian society before meeting her contact later in the evening. She noticed the stares of the businessmen in the bar. They peeked over their laptops or glanced her way occasionally while talking with their business partners or colleagues to get a look at her. She was obviously a Western girl by the way she dressed and held herself. This created a quandary for them. She was attractive, they thought, but should they approach her? She smiled to herself.

Soon her nerves were calm, and she looked at her phone. It was time to go, before she was hit on by the gangster-looking guy across the bar, who was staring at her. She paid the bill and made her way to the exit to flag a taxi. One was waiting, and she hopped in.

"Tverskaya Street," she directed.

The taxi let her out at her direction along the main thoroughfare in Moscow. It was a hot summer day. The Moscow street dust made the heat feel much worse. The cars were coated in a dark brown grime.

Tverskaya Street was in medieval times the connection between the rival cities of Moscow and Tver. Friends at times and enemies at others, the populations over the centuries grew together. Now even many Russians did not know the medieval history of the thoroughfare.

In the United States, old was a few hundred years. Here a few hundred years was a blink of an eye.

Moscow was a dirty city. She had forgotten how much so. She could always tell which Russians had money—they drove the clean cars. They could pay someone to wash their vehicle daily. They also drove like crazy. Traffic laws were not to be obeyed. Many pedestrians were routinely struck and killed traversing the four-lane thoroughfares on the painted crosswalks. Motorists simply didn't slow down. Once the pedestrian walked to the third or fourth lane, they were sitting ducks for the speeding traffic.

If someone was unlucky enough to be pulled over by a policeman, a quick slip of a few thousand rubles took care of any problems.

Wealth was on display everywhere in Moscow. The rich could buy a blue police flashing light to place on top of their car. This gave them the ability to bypass all traffic rules and drive as if they were a cop getting to the scene of an accident. They could be seen all over the roads in the city. They infuriated the "little people" who could not afford such things. One enterprising young Muscovite, sick of the double standard, painted a plastic cup blue and mounted it to the top of his car. He enjoyed disobeying traffic laws for several weeks until he was arrested.

Kate began to walk along the sidewalk. The palatial mansions coexisted with the modernistic shopping areas in harmony. Many of the historical buildings had been destroyed during the revolutionary era, replaced by Stalinist apartment blocks. However, one could feel the age of this place.

She continued walking as with no purpose. Anyone watching her would not know she was waiting for someone. At the last second, she turned and entered an upscale clothing store located on the first floor on the street. She briskly walked through the store and to the rear entrance through the stockroom. She exited into the alleyway behind. There was a darkened sedan waiting. The door opened. She got into the backseat.

"Hello, Kate," said the older Russian man sitting in the backseat. He was handsomely dressed and obviously a man of some stature in life.

"Hello, Vladimir."

"Drive," said the man. The car pulled out swiftly from the alley and disappeared into the traffic.

Kate had developed many relationships during her time previously in Moscow. This man was a source high up in government and inside the Kremlin. He was known to the West as an ally of sorts. He was patriotic but did not like the direction his country was moving in. He was a supporter of democracy and open government. Things were not going his way—in fact, in the other direction. So he had agreed to meet with Kate.

He did not mince words and could not give her much time.

"My government is involved in a plot to reduce the power and influence of the United States globally. We are allied with other powers, primarily the Chinese and Iranians. We ourselves have been arming the Iranians with advanced air defense weaponry in addition to covertly fostering their nuclear program. Our goal is to accomplish what we want primarily through economic means, although there are bound to be a few skirmishes here or there, as you have already seen."

"Tell me why," Kate asked in a firm manner.

"You Americans, in our government's view, have not respected our sphere of influence and have not realized the deep complexes our leaders have regarding the West. You have brought troops to our southern doorstep as well as supported democratic governments in our former territories. We want our sphere back. It's that simple. And the Chinese want Asia, and the Iranians want to control the Middle East. Your government must know all of this already."

Kate looked out the window of the vehicle and thought for a moment. She could tell the sun was beginning to set, even through the darkened glass. It was time to leave. She turned back to Vladimir.

"Thank you for the information. It has been most helpful," she replied.

"Do not contact me again," he added. "I have risked too much already."

The car pulled to the side of the road, and she stepped out into the hot air.

After exiting the vehicle, Kate casually made her way north along Tverskaya Street. She had another appointment that had been set up for her. The sun was beginning to set, but she had plenty of time. In fact, she had time to kill. So she walked slowly, taking in the sights.

The night was starting to come alive. Moscow was a very young city. Youth from all over the Russian Federation came to Moscow to try to find a new life, a life outside of the villages. Lots of well-dressed, beautiful young boys and girls walked the streets, the girls usually in their high heels, the boys in their Italian suits.

She enjoyed the evening air as she contemplated her recent conversation. It was good to see Vladimir again.

Eventually, she arrived at Pushkinskaya metro station and

descended into the underground cavern. It was just as she remembered it.

Moscow had some of the most beautiful metro stations in the world. The architecture was simply stunning. Travelers from New York and other cities in the United States marveled at the style and the cleanliness of the subway in Moscow. In New York, the stations were dirty, run-down, and falling apart in some places. They were downright dangerous. Not in Moscow. Here they were architectural masterpieces.

Pushkinskaya station was designed with substantial white marble columns supporting a vaulted ceiling channeling nineteenth-century style. Grand chandeliers with lights made to look like candles lined the train platform overhead. The look was magnificent.

The station had been one of Kate's favorite places during her previous stay in Moscow, and she enjoyed being back. Architecture was one of her passions.

She boarded the next train and really did not care where it went. Her appointment was not for some time, so she watched the people enter and exit.

At the next stop, she noticed an older woman drop off two small children on the subway car and then leave. The doors closed and the train left the station. One of the little girls was older, maybe nine years of age. A smaller girl lay in her lap, sleeping. She could not have been more than four. They both obviously were very tired, and went right to sleep.

The protective part of Kate kept an eye on them. She couldn't understand how a mother could just leave such small children by themselves. Several stops later, the older girl woke up and shook the smaller child awake. They left the car and made their way to the stairway alone and disappeared. *Strange*, thought Kate. *I guess people here are doing what they can to survive as well. The oligarchs have all the wealth, while the average person struggles.*

She switched trains several times in the next two hours to make sure she was not being followed. When she was satisfied, she took the appropriate train to Teatralnaya station near Red Square in the theater district.

Another masterpiece, again marble walls with ornate stone carvings lining the vaulted ceiling overhead. An art deco checkerboard floor completed the look. *Beautiful*, she marveled.

The sun was gone when she exited the station. There was a crowd of people on the train dressed to see the ballet at the Bolshoi Theatre, which was close by.

The Bolshoi was not Kate's destination.

She went in a different direction and ended up at the Central Universal Magazine, or TSUM, another work of art. It was an enormous shopping mall designed centuries before. It carried all of the toniest brands. Muscovites could buy anything they wanted there, from a designer watch to a small gift for a friend.

Kate made her way to the women's area of one of the clothing stores, and after milling about the floor for a few minutes selected a few things to try on, checked her watch, and headed for the dressing room.

The store was not busy at this time of the day, and the dressing rooms were almost empty. She selected the stall farthest to the rear of the space, closed the door, and sat down to wait.

Fifteen minutes later, she heard the door of the stall next to her open and close. Clothes were hung on the wall. Kate didn't say anything for a while. The walls of the stalls were just louvered slats and very easy to hear through.

Finally, she spoke. "Hello, Natasha."

"*Privyet*, Katarina," the person next to her responded in a thick Russian accent. It was a woman in her late twenties. "It's been a long time," the girl added in fluent English.

143

"Yes it has. It's good to hear your voice again. I have missed you," said Kate with genuine emotion.

"Things are much different now for me than when we knew each other."

"So I am told. Are you here spending his money?"

"Of course! Wouldn't you?"

"I'm sure I would," responded Kate. "When this is all over, let's spend some time together."

"I would like that. I am not allowed now to have many close friends. Especially American agents," she said sarcastically.

"Well let's get down to business," declared Kate. "Do you have any more for us on the Iranian issue?"

"Russia has been arming them. That, I have heard him say. We are not the only country involved. There are others helping us. I am sure your government knows who they are. These are very dangerous times. He means to harm your currency's value. He means to harm your economy with help from these other countries. You must be very careful. However, he has a weakness. He is very worried about the pipelines. I must go now."

"Of course. I will see you soon, my friend. Buy something expensive for me, will you?" quipped Kate.

"I will, my love. *Dasvidania*."

The door opened and Natasha left. Kate waited another ten minutes and then left the store and headed back toward Teatralnaya station.

* * *

The trip back to the Bahamas was long, too long. The layover in New York was extremely frustrating. She was tired of airports.

She had communicated her discoveries to the White House National Security team. She did this immediately upon returning to her hotel room over a secure satellite link. They did not seem surprised. Mainly, the information was confirmation of what they already believed, and it was good to hear the same information from multiple sources.

She had spoken to the president via secure cell phone as well before leaving Russia. When he was briefed on the results of her trip, he asked to speak with her. He was concerned. She laughed it off. Kate was in that phase of youth where she felt invincible, immortal it seemed. She was making significant progress developing intelligence on her country's enemies, and it felt good. Her work in Russia now over, she prepared to make her way back to the Moscow airport.

Kate arrived at the science institute compound late at night on Eleuthera. She was exhausted. She had flown direct into JFK from Moscow and then the direct flight to Nassau, fifteen hours of traveling. The flight from Nassau to Governor's Harbor in Eleuthera was delayed.

"If you have time to spare, fly Bahamas Air," she laughed to herself.

Traveling for that long always gave her a feeling of being wired. She could not relax and definitely couldn't sleep. Not anytime soon anyway.

I'm young; I can handle it, she thought.

She felt better now that the White House was informed of her discussions with her contacts. However, there was still the issue of Connor. She loved him, and that love for him must take her out of his life. Things were too dangerous. He had already lost one love. The thought of not being with him again broke her heart. Connor also was becoming a source for the investigation as well. She could not have further intimate involvement with him. She had risked too much already. He had picked up many pieces of evidence of foreign interference in U.S. national security affairs. She told the president as much.

"It's for the best. I know it," she said to herself.

She thought about calling him but decided against it. Just as she thought of Connor, she received another secure call. She was ordered back to Washington for debriefing. *Well at least it's in the morning*, she thought. She set her alarm clock, lay down on the bed fully clothed, and drifted off to sleep.

* * *

Kate arrived at the new airport in Nassau early the next morning on her way to Washington. The Bahamas had made a big effort recently to bring its infrastructure into the twenty-first century. The shiny new airport was evidence of that. Long gone were the gum-stained floors, congested terminal, and limited parking that were the hallmarks of the old facility.

She needed to meet face-to-face with her superiors, as the investigation was spinning out of control. Maybe a better way to put it was that it was moving above her pay grade. She was sure of herself; it was time to play her ace in the hole after all.

The taxi pulled up to the departure terminal, and she exited and tipped the driver. The taxi sped away. The warm Bahamian breeze was comforting.

She walked up to the Delta ticket counter, and lucky for her, she was early enough and there was not a line.

"Thank God," she muttered as she fished for her passport. Many a day previously she had waited an hour or more to get checked in.

The agent was unusually helpful, and she got her ticket quickly. She then started to haul her bag to customs for the flight into the United States.

The Bahamas was one of the jurisdictions that actually checked passengers through customs into the U.S. while still in-country. That made it easier as they entered the U.S. Passengers could just walk off the plane and blend into the mass of humanity, not having to go through immigration domestically.

She did encounter a line in customs, however, and prepared herself to wait. Her mind began to drift to Connor and their recent time together. It had been magical. She was so confused. She had definitely fallen in love with him. How would she keep this from her chain of command? How would she end it? It was unethical and unprofessional, but it had happened. She would have to find a way to deal with the situation.

The line moved forward.

"Miss," a stern voice behind her said, startling her. "Are you Kate O'Malley?"

"Yes I am, why?"

"Ma'am, please come with us," the husky security officer said as he firmly grasped her arm.

She initially resisted but then relented and was led away from the customs security line and across the check-in terminal. The officer pulled her through a narrow corridor, and they entered a long conference room, where several Bahamian officials were waiting. She was pushed into a waiting chair facing the other occupants of the room.

"Why are you in the Bahamas?" the large, uniformed man asked after a brief moment of silence.

"I'm here conducting research," she proclaimed. "I am sure you know that. What is this about?" She was getting angry.

"We don't believe you," responded an older, plump woman, also uniformed.

"I don't care what you believe." She dared not blow her cover, even in this situation.

"We think you have been stealing jobs from Bahamians!" the woman blurted.

Kate couldn't help but laugh.

"You do, huh? What job was that exactly? I was hired by the scientific institute to come here and conduct research. How is that stealing jobs from the local population?"

"We don't believe you," the large man said. "You are hereby placed under arrest."

Two of the officers in the room then moved forward rapidly and forcibly held her in her seat, while a third cuffed her and then pulled her by the shoulders and stood her up. She couldn't move.

A door opened across the room, and another police officer held it open. The hot Bahamian air billowed into the air-conditioned space. She was led out onto the airport tarmac. A small passenger jet was waiting with engines turning. She was pushed toward the plane.

"Where are you taking me!" she demanded. She met blank stares. "I demand to speak to the U.S. embassy!"

There was no response.

An Asian man came to the open door of the aircraft. She saw the corners of the mouth of one of the guards curl up into a small smile. Then she was really afraid.

Kate was pushed onto the aircraft, which promptly taxied to the main runway for an immediate takeoff.

CHAPTER SIXTEEN

Kingston, Jamaica

Connor left the office building and looked around for his driver. The sun was beating down on him as he left the air-conditioned environment, but it felt good compared to the cold inside. This was a short-lived thrill, however. He began to sweat immediately and took off his jacket. The locals could always tell the briefcase bankers by the suit coats they wore in the heat, businessmen who came to the island for a few days at a time but lived elsewhere. Connor knew this but wore the jacket anyway. He felt naked without it. It had been drilled into him over the course of his career.

His driver was parked down the road and began to return to the building as he saw Connor exit. *Well done, Johann*, he thought. At least his driver was on the ball.

Connor had wrapped up his business in Jamaica and was planning on terminating his trip early. World events were preventing him from staying out of the office any longer. Personal client meetings would have to wait. He was eager to get to the airport.

The car pulled up to the curbside, and Connor opened the door and entered the cool air of the backseat. He used Johann every time he traveled to Kingston, as he was reliable and efficient. Jamaica was one of the few jurisdictions where he allowed himself the luxury of a driver. In less dangerous areas, he was usually found driving with a map pinned to the steering wheel, finding his way around. He actually preferred it that way. He liked to know the terrain he was working in, and refused to use a GPS.

He tried Kate's number on his phone. No answer. He hadn't tried her for several hours, since he had been in meetings all day.

Kate hadn't called. There were no missed calls from her on his phone. She had been due in Washington, D.C., the previous day. Connor was worried. This wasn't like her.

It took thirty minutes to travel the distance to the airport. Kingston was divided into the new and old sections, the newer being constructed to provide a better business environment. It was a little bit safer and more professional, but it was still a challenge to get around without incident, hence the driver.

The check-in at the airport was uneventful. He sat in the terminal in Kingston, waiting for his flight to New York. There were not many others in the gate area, so the flight was most likely not full. He tried Kate again. She wasn't answering her texts either. Something was wrong. He could feel it. The passengers in the waiting area started to stand as the agent began to call for boarding the flight.

Connor made a decision.

He left the departure terminal and went back through security to the ticket counter. The immigration officer gave him dirty looks.

"I want a ticket to Nassau, Bahamas, today!" he told the ticket agent.

It was time to confront Alex.

* * *

New York

Keshwar Rajim was very busy; he was now taking the opposite side of the trade. His biggest client usually came in with bids for the U.S. Treasury auction on a regular basis, very large orders. However, this had stopped completely. Now it had turned around altogether. He was a seller. As they say in the business, a motivated seller.

In the last twenty-four hours, he had sold 300 billion short and long bonds. It had been a challenge for Keshwar to find buyers. There was a buyer's strike.

The thirty-year bond had fallen over ten points in the last few days. Interest rates in the United States were skyrocketing. This would make it extremely difficult for people to buy cars, homes, and other big-ticket items. It would increase costs for business and reduce investment. This in turn would cause employment to stagnate. The economy would drift into a slowdown and an economic recession. A larger and larger amount of the tax revenue of the country would have to be used for paying interest, which would necessitate the need for more borrowing. It was a vicious circle and would crowd out other funding priorities.

For Keshwar it was thrilling. He made money either way. He also didn't care about the consequences to the Americans. It was not his country. He would make enough to exploit the situation for his own gain and then return to India a wealthy man.

The Americans made their own bed, he thought.

He had an idea who was behind his client. Again, he didn't care. He was getting rich executing these trades. Even though his vig was very small on a Treasury sale, the size made up the difference. Keshwar thought of the quote from Groucho Marx, who when asked why he bought Treasury bonds, as one didn't make much money, replied, "You can if you have enough of them."

The Bloomberg terminal alerted him to a new chat coming through.

His client was at it again.

"Sell ten billion ten-year U.S. Treasuries," the message said.

* * *

The only thing Kate knew for sure was that she was on some type of boat. She had been sedated on board the jet and woke up bound and gagged in some type of compartment. Her back hurt, as she could not stand up and stretch. She had no idea how she had gotten there. She could feel the waves rocking the vessel slowly. *It must be very large,* she thought. The sea was not pushing it around.

The one thing she did know was that she was hungry. It had been a long time since she had eaten, but she didn't know how long. And she had to use the bathroom. The plastic ties cut into her wrists and ankles. The drugs were wearing off. Her limbs were asleep. The pain was becoming intolerable.

At some point later in the night, the door opened and she was dragged out of the closet. Under a blindfold, her eyes slowly became accustomed to the light peeking in. She was right; she was on a boat of some sort. Soon after, she was allowed to use the toilet and given some water. The ties on her hands and feet were taken off for this and then replaced.

She was then taken into a stateroom. Her legs gave way beneath her. Whoever was behind her held her up under her shoulders. She could feel the movement of the ocean under her feet, the sound and vibration of the power plant more noticeable now.

She was led to a chair in the middle of the room still blindfolded and tied up again very tightly. Her forearms were fastened to the arms of the chair. The blindfold was abruptly pulled off.

The first thing she noticed was the room. It was very opulent. The second was that she was now alone. Whoever had been there was now gone. It took a while for the sedation to completely wear off. She couldn't recall how long this took, but eventually her faculties returned.

She sat this way for over an hour, or so she guessed. The ties cut deeper into her skin and were very painful.

She was scared, but her resistance training kicked in. Her trainers had prepared her for this. That is, if anything could prepare her for this type of situation. She resolved herself to intense pain and fear. *Once you lose the fear, you can do anything*, she thought.

The door behind her opened.

Someone walked up to her and stood behind her. After a few moments he said in a low, frightening voice, "We want some information." His accent was Asian.

He then reached down and carefully inserted an intravenous tube into her right forearm. Hyoscine-pentothal would cause indescribable pain. The subject would feel as if every nerve ending in the body was on fire. Kate had been administered small doses in the resistance training she received. Large doses could cause death.

She felt the liquid enter her body. Then the pain began. Kate began to scream.

* * *

Nassau, Bahamas

Upon arrival at the airport, Connor rented a car, as he usually did when in the Bahamas. He was driving to the hotel along the highway that led into the city. The vehicle was in better condition than typically was available. The radio worked as well as the air conditioner, and the rattles were kept to a minimum. But he scarcely noticed as he drove along the coast.

It always amazed him how pastel blue the water was in the summer sun. The color contrast to the white beach was striking. Several developers were building homes at the top of the hill abutting the road and the sea, but the houses were far from finished. *They were working on those two years ago*, he thought. *No one's in a hurry here.*

The brand-new walkway along the ocean was crumbling into the sea. That too never changed. The same old potholes filled the road, and the Bahamian feel was as good as ever. *Don't worry, be happy*. He reached over and put on his dark sunglasses to block out the glare. He tried to relax but tensed up again as he thought of Kate. It was no use. He needed to find out what was going on with her.

The Bahamians in the English tradition drove on the left side of the road. The steering wheel was on the opposite side of the car. He had driven in the Bahamas so many times now, he was a natural. *Maybe one day I will build a home here*, he thought.

His phone rang and it startled him. He reached for it lying on the passenger's seat beside him. It was always strange to reach to the left for the passenger's seat but he was more than used to it now after all these years.

"Hello?" he answered.

"This is the White House calling," the operator said. "Please stand by for the president."

Connor was shocked but of course held on. *Has to be a joke*, he thought.

"Connor, this is President Walker," the voice said a few seconds later. "We haven't met, but Kate gave me the run-down on you and what is going on. She works for me, you know."

Connor couldn't decide if this was real or not. He decided to play along. The voice sounded real enough.

"Mr. President, how can I help you?" said Connor.

"Kate's missing," replied the president. "I'd like you to tell my chief of staff everything you know, okay? She has been like a daughter to me."

Connor tensed up in the car. He was aware in the back of his mind that something terrible had happened but did not want to admit it. He had to face the fact now.

"Yes, Mr. President, of course. I have been worried and care for her as well."

"Yes I believe that, Connor. She has told me. That is why I am talking to you. I'd also like you to fly to Washington as soon as possible so we can discuss this in person. We want to debrief you. I'm really concerned about her. I think she is in trouble. I've got some intelligence on this I don't want to discuss over the phone."

"Yes, sir. I will leave tomorrow. I've got some business here I have to attend to first."

He hung up the phone and stared at the sea in desperation. Then he became very angry. He had to confront Alex.

* * *

Connor waited on the deck overlooking the cricket field, sitting at a table on the upper floor of the club. The Bahamian sun was setting, casting a shadow over the arena from Fort Charlotte above him. If the situation were different, he would have enjoyed the scene very much. The local English old men were flirting with the native Bahamian girls serving them. Laughter echoed across the open space. For a moment he let all of his cares go.

He loved it here, in spite of the corruption and in spite of the crime, which was no worse than in the Bronx. The islands were in his blood. He took another swig of his beer and quietly took in the scene. He was waiting on Alex.

Soon he walked up behind Connor.

"Hello, my friend," Alex said. Connor turned around and stood, shaking his hand heartily, not betraying his feelings. Or at least he tried not to. He wanted to read his friend's reaction to seeing him.

"Have a seat, Alex. Let me buy you a beer."

"Of course. I'll let you buy me more than one!" He signaled to the waitress, and she went back inside the bar for his usual drink.

"How's the fishing?" asked Connor.

"Well I may have to start fishing full time, with these markets. I've never seen so much volatility."

"Yes, 'brutal' is a better description. I'm getting too old for this."

It was like old times. For a moment there was no tension between them.

"So how is your lady friend?" Alex asked inquisitively after a few rounds of small talk.

Connor leaned forward in his chair and stared Alex in the eyes for an uncomfortable amount of time. Finally he said, "Why don't you tell me, Alex?"

Alex looked at Connor for a moment and said nothing, but Connor saw something change in his face. His suspicions were correct. Connor knew more than he let on.

"Tell me what's going on, mate!" Connor said again in a feigned closeness.

He was tired of the games.

Alex opened his mouth to speak.

Before he could say a word, an African Bahamian man burst onto the deck from the inside bar. It was the same man who had confronted Alex several weeks before. This time he was wielding a pistol. He ran over towards their table and pointed the handgun at Alex.

"I told you to mind your own tings!" the man shouted, and pulled the trigger.

Alex reacted instinctively but didn't have much time to move. He tried to duck under the metal table and only got so far. The bullet slammed into his shoulder, and he was knocked out of his chair. He fell violently backwards to the ground. He would have survived with just that wound, but the man got off a second shot before Connor tackled him and knocked the weapon out of his hand. They rolled to the floor.

He was strong and probably high on something. Connor couldn't hold him. The man then jumped up and vaulted over the railing of the balcony and slammed into the pavement two stories below. Connor could almost hear his bones crunching as he hit and rolled. In the increasing darkness, he hobbled down to the main thoroughfare below the cricket field and hopped into a waiting car that sped away. Connor watched incredulously. The crowd near the street took no notice.

Stunned, he considered following him but decided otherwise. He turned back to his friend. The bar patrons had fled the balcony. They were alone.

Alex was lying prone on his back. A pool of blood lay under his shoulders and was dripping from his nose and mouth.

"Call an ambulance!" Connor screamed to the bartender inside the club.

He lifted Alex's head and rolled him onto his stomach. There was a huge exit wound from the round right where his kidney should have been. He was not going to make it.

He looked at Alex.

"Why?" he asked. There was so much he didn't understand.

"You are American," Alex whispered, and spit blood at the same time. "You wouldn't understand. You have had everything you have always wanted, and when you don't get your way, you just take it. Well, things are changing."

He coughed more blood and rested for a couple of seconds, trying to regain his strength.

"I saw my parents lose everything! My father was a Communist Party official. KGB, for God's sake, and was well respected. When the Soviet Union collapsed, I saw him beg for a job to be a common laborer. We were humiliated. My mother had to clean toilets! So yes, I have helped my country and others try and find your gold! Gold will be all that is worth anything. Your dollar will be worth less than the paper it's printed on. It's already too late for you. You have borrowed too much. America is finished!" Alex was angry to the end.

"Who else is involved?" asked Connor.

Alex was having trouble breathing now. The wail of the ambulance could be heard, but it was still far away.

"China, Russia, Iran," whispered Alex.

Connor knew Alex was dying, so he pushed for more information. The answers were coming only in short, almost silent, whispers.

"They have started a war to bankrupt you."

"Then why did they try to kill you?"

"Not them, the prime minister, for money," whispered Alex, and then he went silent.

"Where is Kate?" Connor asked one last question.

Alex could no longer respond. He was dead.

Connor stood and looked out over the field and the coming darkness. The angst inside him was unbearable.

Where is she? What do I do now? he thought.

* * *

Hours later he sat alone. He had given his statement to the police late at night downtown at the Nassau station. He didn't expect they would be much help. They didn't seem that concerned about the situation. Money had changed hands. No one was talking.

He was still in shock that his friend Alex was gone. He was also stunned at how little he knew about the man. That was obvious now. Connor's world was changing. He didn't know what to expect next. The worst part of it was that he had been unable to extract any information on Kate's whereabouts. Connor was beside himself with worry.

Soon he was driving back to the hotel. Deciding he was hungry, he stopped at one of the few gourmet restaurants in town, tucked behind the parliament building. The owner recognized him.

"You don't look so good," said the owner. "Can I help you with anything?"

"Just a quiet table, my friend, but thank you."

His friend led him to an open courtyard in the middle of the restaurant, and to a private table. The building was old, and the vines grew up the brick walls of the courtyard towards the sky. The few patrons remaining were enjoying themselves, and the wine was flowing. It was a peaceful setting.

Connor needed some peace. He needed to relax. He needed to clear his mind.

The waitress brought water, and he ordered a bottle of cabernet. He needed to calm down and think. The weight of the day's events sunk into him, and his shoulders slumped. The wine helped a little bit.

"I have to think this through!" he said aloud to no one.

He asked the waitress for pen and paper and started to write down what he knew. He had to make sense of everything that was happening.

Alex had obviously been double-dealing. He said the prime minister had killed him. Was that because he was looking for gold for the alliance? And the Bahamian government wanted it? Connor was aware of the brutal way of doing business in the Bahamas. One of his business colleagues had been murdered after he had filed charges against an ex-minister of parliament, who had stolen money from his company. That part was understandable. It was the way things worked here. What he didn't understand was the blatant nature of the killing. Were they trying to send a message to the other entities looking for the gold? *Anything is possible*, he thought.

And then there was Kate. His stomach turned in knots as he thought of her. He could do nothing, and felt helpless. She needed him. He could feel it. He gulped the wine. The next plane out was the next day, midmorning. Connor's personal assistant had arranged that. The trip to D.C. would have to wait. Tomorrow was another day. His thoughts turned to more global matters.

So if China, Russia, and Iran were in on the scheme, hence the reason for the recent hostilities in the Persian Gulf. They must have known they could not stand up to the American Navy. Connor stewed on this fact for a while and took another sip of wine. His food arrived.

The answer came to him in a flash of insight. They did not need to win the conflict. They just needed to tie down the American military and make them spend resources they did not have. *Ingenious*, he thought.

And the bond market was going crazy. Their plan was working. Interest rates were through the roof, and the cost for the United States was unsustainable. The war was forcing them to borrow even more money. It was maddening.

He needed to get to Washington and find out what the government knew, but he could do nothing now.

He also needed to tell the president and his staff his insights into what was going on. His country was in danger, and the clock was ticking. Connor hardly slept during the ensuing night.

* * *

Washington, D.C.

He reached Reagan National early afternoon the next day, having taken the midmorning flight from Nassau through Atlanta. On the plane, Connor was consumed with worry for Kate. The feeling of helplessness brought back memories. It reminded him of Emily. He pushed the thoughts out of his mind. *Not now*, he told himself.

He had been told that he would be met, and he indeed he was. He exited the jetway and was immediately greeted by two anonymous security personnel in gray suits, who then asked him to follow. He did as he was instructed.

Secret Service, he mused.

They led him to a waiting black Suburban, which had the official prerogative to wait at curbside outside the arrival terminal as opposed to the average, ordinary citizen who was shooed away by the police if they stopped for ten seconds. He felt privileged. The men inside said not a word. He helped himself to the bottled water that was chilled in the backseat.

The trip to the White House was quick and painless. It tended to be that way, because they didn't have to obey traffic laws and could turn on the flashing red and blue lights at their convenience. They flew at a high rate of speed down the highway into the city. Soon they were at the White House gate and showing their identification.

The vehicle was searched and then allowed through to the entrance gate of the iconic structure. It was Connor's second time, and he had to admit he was still awed. The building was majestic.

The door to the SUV was opened for him by a Marine guard in a painfully starched uniform. Connor quickly exited the vehicle and walked the short distance to enter the president's home as the same Marine opened the front door.

He had been at the White House years before for a fundraiser, but this time the access was much more informal. After passing through security, he was led down a long corridor into a briefing room and seated alone at a large conference table. Slowly the president's staff came in. The introductions were short and sweet. Then everyone stood as the president himself walked into the boardroom.

He was a handsome, confident, and impressive man. He exuded an aura of command. Halfway through his first term, the man had settled into the office. The president shook Connor's hand vigorously.

"Connor," the president said after the introductions, "thank you for coming on such short notice. Kate contacted me a few days ago and wanted me to meet with you. This was prior to her disappearance. She seemed to think you had information and had experienced some things that might be of help in our analysis of this situation. Please tell my people here everything you can think of."

"Of course, Mr. President."

The president's chief of staff then asked Connor several specific questions to divulge what he knew about Kate and what could have happened to her. Connor quickly revealed all he could remember, including the details about what had been transpiring over the last few weeks and what had been happening with Kate and Alex. He made special mention of his last conversation with Alex and Kate's suspicions of him.

He noticed eyes go up and acknowledging looks across the table when he mentioned the Iran War and the alliance goals.

"Alex has been working for this alliance of nations attempting to hurt us economically," the national security advisor stated. "The alliance is after Hamilton's gold. So was the Bahamian prime minister. It was his men who shot Alex. They feared losing the gold to the Chinese."

Connor mentioned he had feared as much.

When he was done, the president stood and shook his hand.

"Thank you for coming in, Connor," he stated. "I will do everything I can to get Kate home. These people are going to further debrief you now. You have my staff's number if you think of anything else. Again, thank you for the service to your country, and I will be in touch."

Connor spent the next two hours answering questions with lower-ranked personnel and then was free to leave. He left the White House in a worried mood and with a sick feeling in his stomach.

* * *

Oval Office

President Walker stared out the window behind his desk towards the Rose Garden. The grounds were spectacular. It always amazed him how the staff kept flowers in bloom almost year-round, constantly rotating plants as their flowers died off to different species. His mind drifted back to the problems at hand, and he turned back to his desk.

The Resolute desk in the Oval Office was a beautiful, ornate piece. It was a gift from Queen Victoria in 1880 to the United States, built from the timbers of the British Arctic explorer HMS *Resolute*. It had been used by many presidents before him. That thought gave him comfort during these trying times. He hoped it would impart wisdom to him in some way.

He was very concerned about Kate and feared the worst. He wondered how he would tell his daughter. She would be beside herself if Kate were harmed. They were so close.

He was also very concerned about another woman. She was a mole deep in the Kremlin who was feeding U.S. intelligence information for some time now about the alliance's intentions. Besides the president, only the director of the Central Intelligence Agency and her handlers knew of her existence. She was very deep.

The president had been forewarned in a vague way by her as to what forces were arrayed against the United States across the world, but he had not expected the hostilities in the Gulf.

The world was getting very dangerous.

Code name "Incredible" was also in grave danger. All the president knew was that she was female. He also knew she was invaluable to the United States. However, sources were informing her CIA handlers that she was close to being discovered. The Russian Federal Security Service, or FSB, was aware there was a mole in their midst. They were actively searching for the source of leaks to Western intelligence.

President Walker made the decision. It was time to get her out, as his advisor had suggested. He turned around to his desk and picked up the phone.

"Get me the director of the CIA," he said to his assistant.

CHAPTER SEVENTEEN

Washington, D.C.

The president sat with his national security staff in the Situation Room at the White House. The mood was tense. The Strait of Hormuz had been closed in the Persian Gulf. Energy prices were skyrocketing. It would take time for the military to get naval and air assets in place to deal with the situation.

The Situation Room had been built by President Kennedy to provide a secure place for the president to control United States forces around the world with real-time information. Located under the West Wing, the facility was staffed by over thirty agency representatives twenty-four hours a day to provide the most up-to-date information anywhere in the world to enable the president to make informed decisions.

And today there were decisions to be made.

"Mr. President," the national security advisor started the conversation, "we have evidence the Russians have been supplying weapons to the Iranians in the Gulf. We have evidence the Chinese and the Russians have been buying gold reserves worldwide. We have known for years they both have been active off our shores in the Caribbean as well as globally buying economic and political influence. We also have strong communications intelligence there has been active coordination in multiple areas among Russia, China, and Iran prior to the attack in the Gulf. There have also been coordinated attempts to drive up our interest rates to harm the economy. They are using their substantial ownership of U.S. debt as a weapon."

"Obviously we have a multilateral effort here, as we suspected," the president concluded. "They are attempting to weaken this country where she is most vulnerable, our economy. If they can drive up our rates and make our debt unsustainable while concurrently driving us deeper into debt with military spending, eventually we will become less of a power militarily and politically as well. What I want now is options! We have a coordinated attack against the economic viability of the United States. From this point on I consider us on a war footing."

"We should respond in kind, Mr. President," the secretary of defense noted. "Iran should be dealt with militarily. Russia and China, economically."

"I agree," the president responded. "I have been thinking the same thing."

The United States was going to war again.

"We have to be strong here, people. Weakness is what got us into this situation. I hate to say it, but people need to be scared of the United States, of her power and her will to use it. I want options on destroying the military capability of Iran. I don't care what it costs. We will get this economy going again and deal with the expenses. It's the most resilient economy in the world. I want my people to be safe."

The staff was furiously taking notes.

"I also want economic options to deal with Russia and China. I have ideas in mind myself," he added.

* * *

A curious system developed in international finance over the last several decades. As the wealthy were asked to pay more and more of the tax burden in the developed and developing markets, they naturally gravitated towards finding solutions to avoid paying these higher taxes and preserve their wealth. This happened in the corporate world as well. This circumstance was the catalyst behind the development of a plethora of offshore financial jurisdictions that operated as tax havens and, among other purposes, confidentiality and asset protection.

These typically were established on islands in warm climates. This made the board of directors meetings so much more pleasurable. The quintessential offshore tax haven was the Caribbean with its many remote and almost isolated islands. One of the sleepiest of these was Nevis, located down the Western Indies chain towards South America.

The main town of Charleston was established right on the edge of the water towards its sister island of St. Kitts. The infrastructure of the port consisted of a concrete pier jutting out into the ocean and a crumbling seawall protecting the ramshackle buildings up against the sea. The caldera of the long-dormant volcano rose behind the town. It was the perfect scene for a thriller novel.

* * *

The SEAL team was most concerned with one of these buildings. The small submarine drifted slowly towards the harbor in the middle of the night, coming within 250 yards of the seawall while stealthily traveling fifty feet under the surface. The dredged harbor provided the depth needed to operate the vessel. The crew skillfully navigated as close to the target as possible.

The hatch on top of the submarine opened, and five SEALs exited in scuba gear and motored underwater with small propellant devices towards the water barrier in the harbor. They covered the small distance in a short period of time.

Their target was one of the nondescript office buildings located across the road from the edge of the land facing the water. There were tourist shops on the street level with office space located above. T-shirts and small trinkets adorned the windows below. There was a bar on the end of the small commercial building, but at this late hour it was empty. Advertisements for the local brewery fluttered in the night wind off the ocean. Broken glass littered the parking lot next door, evidence of the prior night's activities.

The frogmen arrived at the base of the pier and stowed their craft for later use, hiding them under the waterline. They then removed their gear, stowed it as well, and silently made their way towards the office building. Under cover of darkness, they slowly and stealthily climbed up the stairs to the outside hallway facing the ocean. No one was in sight.

* * *

One of the classic offshore schemes to provide confidentiality and asset protection was to set up a corporation in a jurisdiction that would conduct business only outside of its geographic location. These typically were called international business corporations, or IBCs. They usually paid no tax to their domicile and were legally protected by the jurisdiction's legislative code. Most of the jurisdictions were forced to share tax data with the U.S. and other countries, but that did not hinder their privacy or confidentiality capabilities. Many governments resented this competition for their tax dollars. It was not so easy to strip-mine the residents of a country to feed the government when there was an outlet for the person or corporation to move and reduce its tax load. There was a concerted effort by international regimes to rein in this competition, and it had worked to some extent, but the tax havens still existed and even thrived.

The Organization for Economic Co-operation and Development, or OECD, was a group of thirty-four developed economies whose principal aim was to foster sound economic policies among its members. It had been created after WWII to administer the Marshall Plan in Europe. In the past decade this organization had maintained a "blacklist" of jurisdictions that did not provide tax transparency and exchange of tax information with member countries. They had threatened to cut off access to the international banking system if their targets did not conform to their demands. However, many new havens sprang up over the years in this never-ending battle.

Each of these financial domiciles could have hundreds or even thousands of companies operating inside its borders. They typically were run by a staff consisting of hired management and a mercenary board of directors. Some of these individuals sat on the boards of hundreds of companies. It was a shell game of course, but it worked for the purposes of the underlying beneficiary.

* * *

The building that the SEALs targeted housed one of these management companies. The offices of not less than forty-six IBCs made their home in this building at the West Indies Management Company, Inc. One of their companies was sending orders via West Indies personnel in Nevis to sell large amounts of United States Treasury bonds to their bond traders in New York and other places. The traders knew it was a shell company but didn't ask questions. As far as they were concerned, they were making too much money. Besides, their firm had done their due diligence; they were protected legally. Or at least they hoped.

The commandos made their way silently down the outdoor corridor to the upstairs office entrance quickly and quietly. Forcefully they entered the office. The team began thoroughly searching the premises and confiscated several hard drives, thumb drives, and reams of paper from the location. The operation took less than thirty minutes and was unobserved by anyone on the island. The precious cargo, or PC, was then protected in waterproof containers.

As silently as they had come, they made their way back to their equipment and walked into the ocean.

* * *

Midtown Manhattan

Keshwar Rajim was happy. He sat as his terminal, looking over his previous day's commissions. He had become a very wealthy man. In the last twenty-four hours, he had padded that wealth by five hundred thousand dollars. Life was good. He thought of the new Ferrari he had just ordered. He had just walked into the showroom on Park Avenue and paid cash, three hundred thousand dollars. He couldn't wait for it to be delivered.

How many other thirty-year-olds could do that? he asked himself. The funny thing was, the salesman had not been surprised. *Such was life on Wall Street*, Keshwar reasoned.

His big client in Nevis had been extremely busy. There were repeated orders to sell U.S. Treasuries, and he had done a good job of getting his client the best price possible. Success brought more success. He was a master of the universe. In other Wall Street jargon, a big swinging dick! He noticed the respect his superiors were showing him. He had arrived. The only thing they respected was money.

He was on top of the world.

What he did not realize was that from there, he could only look into the abyss.

* * *

It was ten o'clock in the morning when they strode onto the trading floor. The floor was busy and loud with shouting, but it quickly muted as everyone saw them enter. The CEO of the firm escorted them in and led them to Keshwar's seat.

The floor was now silent. Ten men clothed in FBI jackets tended to do that.

"Keshwar Rajim?" one of the agents asked.

"Yes," said Keshwar, initially shocked and now frightened.

"FBI. You are under arrest. Put your hands above your head!"

Of course Keshwar did as he was told. He was tender at heart and had never had the courage in his life to confront anyone. It was not in his nature. And it certainly was not going to happen now.

He complied with the directive and was quickly handcuffed and led off the floor, down the elevator, and into a waiting car.

He was then taken to a secret CIA interrogation center in New York City. They mined him for a week for what he knew, and then he was deported back to India.

He never entered the United States again.

* * *

Somewhere in the Caribbean Sea

The pilot flipped the switch, and the auxiliary power unit, or APU, began to whine in the dark of the night as the aircraft came to life. The sound created an odd comparison to the natural noises of the sea around them and the low rumbling of the ship. Connor sat in the rear of the aircraft cabin sandwiched in between some rather rough-looking characters.

He could see through the opening between the pilots to the cockpit, where the flight engineer would soon be sitting; the lights on the instrument panel began to flicker. The pilots were busy going through their processes. Constant short, staccato bursts of human voices permeated his headset from the multiple radio frequencies involved in the mission. The vibration of the small turbine engine of the APU felt like an insect buzzing under his seat. The sound was muted by his helmet and the earplugs he had been given.

Although they were dressed in battle gear, he could still make out the muscled strength beneath the black fatigues of the warriors around him. The green glow of the night vision cabin lights created an eerie scene. The thing he noticed most, however, was their blank stare; it cut right through him, like a dead zone through his heart. Many had beards, some ponytails. They would never be recognized as members of the U.S. Navy's most elite counterterrorism team, SEAL Team Six. They would fit in on any street worldwide. Of course, that was the plan.

They had endured brutal training for years, which was not survivable for most men. But these were not normal men. They were the best of the best. The finest group of commandos the world could produce. He felt like a dwarf around them; he was just an observer. They tolerated him, respectfully asking him to just stay out of their way.

President Walker had offered the favor of letting him ride on the mission. The president loved Kate as well, like a daughter. Connor very much appreciated the gesture. He had taken him up on it, and here he was. Adrenaline raced through his body.

The aircraft were parked on the deck of the USS *Bataan*, an amphibious assault ship. This vessel was specifically designed to support helicopter-borne assaults. In fact, she was the ship that had initially tested the viability of the MV-22 tiltrotor for naval operations.

There were four U.S. Air Force CV-22 Ospreys from the U.S. Air Force Special Operations Command and six MH-60K Black Hawks from the U.S. Army 160th Special Operations Aviation Regiment lined up on the deck. The Ospreys were filled with commandos from ST6 and an Air Force Pararescue medical team. Connor was located in one of these aircraft. Inside the Black Hawks were more ST6 snipers and two command modules with appropriate personnel, including the airborne mission commander. Linguists were also on board to monitor communications from the target. There were also backup aircraft and teams available in case the worst happened.

This mission had been rehearsed in detail and every possibility thought of. The JSOC, Joint Special Operations Command, had leased a similar vessel and the strike team had been practicing on it for a week. They had attempted to refine their tactics and get the assault package familiar with this type of operation. Now that the mission was a go, there was an eerie calm. They had trained as hard as they could, and now there was nothing to do but execute.

The National Security Agency had been tracking the white yacht for months now and currently had its location plotted out to sea one hundred miles south of the Bahamas, steaming eastbound. There was very strong circumstantial evidence from this surveillance that Kate had been taken on board the yacht. The occupants had little idea that this would be their last night on the vessel.

The Black Hawks were slower than the Ospreys, so they were scheduled to leave first. To the second, the auxiliary power units of the aircraft started together, the whine sounding like a warning siren in a small town. The cockpits were dimmed, and the pilots lowered and turned on their night vision goggles. Small ChemLights with only a pinhole showing through were taped to the pilots' fingers, so they could simply point to anywhere in the cockpit and see what was needed. Even that small amount of light lit up the cockpit while flying on the light-sensitive goggles. It was a no-moon night, as the pilots called it, with an overcast sky, so any amount of light would help.

A no-moon night, the better to surprise you with, thought Connor.

Checklists were run through, guns were checked, and final walk-arounds by the flight engineers were completed. Each item was completed with precision by each aircraft at the exact same instant, per the mission timeline. Fifteen minutes later to the second, six rotors began turning. The noise was deafening. A complicated dance was played out as each crew member and team leader executed their radio checks and other items in perfect synchronicity. Then the flight of six aircraft rose to a hover. They departed the ship and dove towards the deck of the black, rolling sea. The lead aircraft directed the flight, and the remaining aircraft followed its every move.

Flying at night over water with no illumination on night vision goggles was a challenging feat indeed. The pilots had no depth perception and relied on radio altimeters, terrain-following radar, and the crew's vision to prevent them from flying into the water. There was no margin for error flying at almost two hundred miles an hour at twenty feet over the water at night. Low altitude was essential to prevent radar detection from the target. If the first aircraft flew into the water, the rest of the flight would most likely crash as well.

"Red flight whiskey," the flight lead stated tersely over the secure radio channel to the overall mission commander located on board the carrier. "Whiskey" was the code word for the flight having departed to the target. Although they were using secure radio and satellite communication, all messages were extremely brief and encoded with predetermined words.

The mission commander was a one-star general from the Joint Special Operations Command. His task was to control all of the moving parts of this complicated dance and ensure the success of the operation. He had video feeds from each aircraft as well as helmet-mounted cameras on each assault team member. All of the video was simultaneously transmitted to the Situation Room at the White House.

Each of the lives of the troops under his command this evening weighed on the officer greatly. However, the success of the mission was paramount for the country and superseded any personal feelings he might have towards his troopers. He would sacrifice their lives if needed for mission success. It was understood by everyone involved. After all, everyone here tonight had volunteered for this special duty.

Five miles into the sky, a lumbering, gray, blacked-out C-17 specially outfitted for special operations slowly lowered its rear ramp. She was a huge beast. The flight engineers and loadmasters checked their cargo and the chutes one more time. The aircraft had slowed to just above stall speed.

The copilot at the appropriate time flipped a switch, and the night vision–compatible warning light illuminated the cabin. The loadmaster flashed a thumbs-up to the team leader and hit the lever to release the cargo.

The large SEAL fast attack boat silently fell out of the back of the aircraft. The team members were deployed in the boat at the time, equipped with oxygen masks. The craft fell for twenty-five thousand feet before the chutes popped open and broke the fall of the vessel. The oxygen masks were removed, and the power systems on the boat were initiated. The boat splashed into the sea with the engine running, and the chutes were released. Two more boats splashed down nearby, having fallen from different aircraft in the formation. The craft were specially constructed to emit very little noise, stealth if you will.

They formed up together and silently headed to the target area.

The last aircraft to depart were the CV-22s. Built as a hybrid between a rotary-wing aircraft and a fixed-wing, they were very versatile aircraft. Six glass instrument panels adorned the futuristic cockpit. Every bit of data needed—aircraft performance, threat information, communications, navigation, et cetera—was perfectly transmitted to the crew in a very efficient way. The Osprey provided extremely unique capabilities, such as self- deployment, range, and speed. However, there were some drawbacks as well. The blast from the large rotors during hover was difficult for the offloading troops to handle. The aircraft was also very complicated and new. As with all new military aircraft, there were problems to be worked out.

They departed blacked out as well, turned the engine nacelles forward, and quickly achieved close to 250 knots across the ocean surface, the pilots also using a mixture of electronics and vision to fly the aircraft. Connor was in the lead aircraft.

All of the aircraft and boats converged on the target.

"One minute out!" the pilot of the lead CV-22 called over the intercom to the team leader in the rear. The SEALs stood, released their safety harnesses and began their final equipment checks.

I can't believe I'm seeing this, thought Connor as he marveled at the precision with which these people operated.

The formations moved to the rear of the yacht five miles in trail and began closing the distance. This was to minimize the chances of radar detection. Most civilian scopes had a dead zone to the rear of their coverage.

They began closing the distance at a high rate of speed. The boats were the slowest but had the shortest distance to go. The flight of Black Hawks was next and then the CV-22s. All of the aircraft and fast boats converged on the yacht at the same time plus or minus five seconds. In fact all of the aircraft as well were silently modified for stealth, and no one heard them coming.

The boats came alongside the yacht and hoisted grappling hooks to the upper deck. At that exact moment, the Black Hawks, two by two port and starboard of the ship, came alongside. They flared the helicopters abruptly to slow their rapid rate of forward speed, and their noses pitched into the air. At the same time, the pilots reduced power to a minimum. The helicopters stopped on a dime.

Snipers with silencers were sitting sideways in the open doors, secured with gunner's belts. They began firing at any moving target on deck or that was able to be seen inside. Ten seconds later, two CV-22s began fast-roping commandos onto the deck of the yacht, one on the bow and one on the stern.

The element of surprise being gone, the emphasis now was on preventing anyone on board from destroying evidence or harming hostages. The commandos swarmed the deck, taking out shooters and sprinting down to the decks below. Although it looked chaotic, everything was done in a very methodical fashion.

Kate lay in a closet on the lower deck, bound and gagged. She had been interrogated and tortured repeatedly using chemicals. Her body was suffering but she did not whimper. She heard the firing above, and in her dreamy state due to lack of sleep, she tried to awaken.

The door was yanked open and she was pulled from her cell. Her legs failed her and she soiled herself. She was embarrassed. She had been holding it for so long and couldn't anymore. Her rescuer didn't seem to care.

"It's okay," he whispered. "Don't worry about it. We'll take care of it soon."

She felt herself being carried swiftly above deck. Whoever was carrying her was very strong and kind.

The sound of gunfire died down; only the occasional shot was heard as she felt the fresh air of the sea as she arrived on the deck of the ship. She vaguely recognized the fuzzy outline of some type of aircraft that had landed on the helipad on the stern. The large rotors on each wing were still turning, and it was very loud. The stars suddenly showed themselves above as the overcast layer cleared. There were thousands of points of light above her. She felt herself frozen in time as she tried to count them all. It was impossible, she knew.

The sound grew louder as her rescuer neared the aircraft. She felt herself being lifted into the cabin. The lights above were extinguished, and all she could make out was an eerie green glow. However, she knew there were people all around her, tending to her. She felt poked and probed. Her soiled clothes were taken off. She didn't care. A warm covering was placed over her.

She looked up and saw her new friend. She could make out his smile. The smile told her she was okay.

Everything went black as she passed out on the litter inside the cabin of the CV-22. The U.S. Air Force Special Operations Pararescue team was frantically tending to her medical needs. The aircraft rose vertically into the air and drifted away from the ship. The nacelles on the wings turned slowly forward. The aircraft then deliberately began moving from a hover to an ever-increasing forward airspeed. She was free.

Two other patients were on the aircraft with her. Two of the SEALs had been wounded in action. One had been shot in the throat and was terminal. The other had just a large flesh wound in the thigh and was bleeding heavily. He would survive, but his colleague died in the medics' hands. Kate was oblivious to it all.

* * *

Connor did not fast-rope to the deck with the commandos at the start of the raid. He stayed in the cabin of the CV-22 and watched the mission unfold through the green glow of his night vision goggles. The gunner's belt around his waist allowed him to move around the cabin unhindered, but he was restricted from exiting the aircraft by the thick, webbed fabric similar to a large seat belt in an automobile.

The aircraft once disgorged of troops had moved to a hover off the side of the ship with a full range of view of the happenings from the open door of the cabin. Gunfire erupted from the vessel, and his helmet was filled with the short, disciplined, staccato bursts of communication from the actors in this elaborate dance.

The deck looked like an ant bed as the commandos scurried around prosecuting their assigned tasks. But Connor was not focused on this. He strained his eyes to look for Kate.

Then he saw her.

Two SEALs emerged from a hatch. The latter carried the prostrate form of a female. She seemed delirious. The SEAL sprinted across the deck to the medical aircraft, which had landed on the helipad at the stern of the vessel.

The girl then raised her head and looked at the sky.

Connor looked up and saw the arrangement of stars splattered across the heavens. It was beautiful. He was moved by the sight of her discovering so much beauty while in the obvious state of distress that she found herself in.

Well that's my Kate, he thought. Always the optimist.

The commando almost threw her into the aircraft. Behind him was another group of soldiers carrying wounded comrades. They carefully handed their wounded brethren to the waiting Pararescue medics and backed away.

With the commotion inside after receiving such cargo, the CV-22 lifted into a momentary hover. It dove to the sea and increased speed as it moved away from the ship.

The remaining troops on the ship completely cleared the vessel. They spent the better part of two hours taking apart the ship and retrieving any intelligence possible. Any occupants left alive were taken off the ship for interrogation. The vessel was then supplied with a new crew and steamed towards an undisclosed location for further analysis.

The Osprey was sprinting now at 250 knots of airspeed at low level across the surface of the ocean. The destination was the USS *Bataan* from whence she had started. The crew was sad about the loss of their fellow warrior but was focused on their patients left alive, male and female. They were fifteen minutes out from the assault carrier.

The Osprey had many unique capabilities due to its unique design and hybrid nature between a fixed-wing aircraft and a helicopter. It allowed teams to be inserted and extracted in confined areas with a much greater range than normal rotary-wing aircraft.

However, this capability came at a price. This was a very

complicated machine mechanically, and not all the kinks had been worked out yet. Such was the case with all experimental aircraft that were operationally fielded, no matter the amount of testing that had been accomplished.

Many a flight manual of now commonplace aircraft was filled with "notes, cautions, and warnings" that were discovered and paid for with blood and treasure.

This was now one such case.

The hydraulics on the Osprey were quite complicated. Although the engineers had attempted to anticipate every possibility, this was impossible. On the starboard wing of the medical aircraft, the pressure in one of the hydraulic tubes became too great at this high rate of speed. The designers had simply made a bad calculation and had not provided enough margin of error in the strength of the tubing. In most cases there would not have been a problem, but due to the rough weather and the high rate of speed and an unknown defect in the metal, the tube failed.

It is said that a helicopter pilot is a nervous individual because he knows that his aircraft is held together by opposing forces, and anything that upsets this balance will cause a catastrophe.

Well this was one of those moments.

The failure of the hydraulic line meant that the engine nacelle was now free to travel around its attaching point, and it immediately gravitated towards the path of least resistance, which was upwards away from the oncoming airflow at over two hundred nautical miles an hour, or knots.

This caused an asymmetrical thrust situation on the two wings of the aircraft. In other words, the plane spun out of control.

Since the engine was now pointed upwards on the starboard wing, this wing flipped upwards, and the port wing was pushed down into the ocean.

The wingtip grazed the ocean surface, and that was all she

wrote. The aircraft cartwheeled across the waves until settling upside down and quickly sank.

Everyone on board was killed instantly due to the forces involved. That was the only consolation.

CHAPTER EIGHTEEN

New York

The Russian president confidently mounted the podium at the United Nations. The chamber was silent, and the members waited patiently. They expected an important speech. At least that was what was billed. He paused as his hands gripped the side of the podium and looked out at the audience for effect. He resembled a Southern preacher ready to deliver God's judgment to his congregation.

"Mr. President of the General Assembly of the United Nations, Mr. Secretary-General of the United Nations, Excellencies, Ladies and Gentlemen," he began as he paid his respects to the officials present. Although fluent in English, he spoke in Russian.

"The Russian Federation has long felt that we were playing on an unfair playing field regarding trade. One of the reasons is that most international trade is conducted in United States dollars. I am here to announce that Russia has joined with other great nations to replace the U.S. dollar as the global reserve and trading currency. We, in conjunction with our partners, are establishing a new global currency that will be based on a basket of sovereign currencies. Russia, China, and others will no longer use the U.S. dollar for trade payments."

There was a low murmur among the members of the chamber.

Then someone started clapping. Then the chamber for the most part erupted in applause. The members of the United Nations had long been anti-American, even as America paid twenty-five percent of the United Nations' dues. The American delegation as well as her remaining allies got up from their seats and walked out of the chamber. They had expected as much of a declaration.

He continued, "For too long, the United States has enjoyed lower interest rates and an irrationally high currency valuation. This has resulted in a higher standard of living, due to the demand that a reserve currency creates. This will now end. The United States will have to compete with the rest of the world for capital on an equal footing."

The Russians had brought up this single world currency idea six years ago, but now the issue was a reality, at least for part of the world. Since the USD would no longer be used as a global reserve currency by many nations, there would not be so much demand for the dollar. Therefore the United States would have to pay higher interest rates to attract buyers of its debt. Again, the United States debt situation was completely out of control, and this rise in rates was unsustainable. But of course, this was entirely the plan.

From the seventeenth to nineteenth centuries, the global currency was the Spanish piece of eight, based on precious metals. Then the Spanish empire decayed from within. The empire's many wars depleted her treasury even after the trillions of gold and silver were brought back to her shores.

As the British Empire flourished, the world shifted to the pound sterling. London became the financial capital of the world. This lasted until the end of World War II. Fighting the Nazi war machine was a financial mountain too great to climb, even after the Marshall Plan.

Once the British began to lose their empire after that great global conflict, the world shifted to the United States dollar as the global reserve currency. The impact of British debt from the world wars caused the sterling to weaken and hurried along the process. The British simply could no longer afford their empire or protect it. The Bretton Woods Conference at the end of World War II established the USD as the global trading currency, one that was based on a link to gold. When President Nixon took the U.S. dollar off the gold standard in the early seventies, the USD became a fiat global reserve currency.

Russia and China had set up a system of expanding the International Monetary Fund, or IMF, Special Drawing Rights (SDR) and based the new currency on a basket of world currencies, which included the USD. This, however, was no help in reducing the extremely negative impact of this development on the United States and its ability to survive as an economic power.

The Russian president spoke with a smile on his face.

Gold hit a new high on global markets.

* * *

September 14, 1836
Port Richmond, New Jersey

He knew it was coming. He welcomed it. In fact, he yearned for it. He could feel the change happening within his body, the organs shutting down. He hoped he would like what was in store for him. But he didn't care; he just wanted it to happen. The pain here was too great. Today was the day. He knew it.

Theodosia was gone. His wife had left him. He was disgraced. That was the pain he could not bear, that his country had lost faith in him. The country he had helped birth. The country he had fought for.

The clergy had stopped coming. He was thankful for that. They had been trying to redeem his soul. His soul didn't need redeeming, in his mind. It was all a bunch of hogwash. What he needed was to be left alone.

He was bitter, a misanthrope. It felt good to him, to hold the bitterness. It was what had kept him alive the last few years.

Aaron Burr lay in his bed. Earlier in the day he had picked up one of the letters strewn around the room from his many women. The author was special to him. He remembered her touch, the way she captivated him. He missed her. He hadn't seen her for years. Her jealous husband had seen to that. But oh, she was so beautiful in his memory.

One of many.

He hadn't left this room in the boarding house for weeks now. It was his deathbed. That he knew.

How he hated the human race. His life should have turned out so differently.

But alas, it was not to be.

He was penniless. He was alone. He was dying.

The irony was that today his divorce was final. The woman who was so fond of him, until he had spent half her fortune on bad land deals, was no longer to be his wife. An extremely wealthy widow, Eliza Jumel loved him but could not be with him. She even nursed him through sickness after she left him but would never be with him again.

The women all ran together. They loved him but in the end left him. It was his burden. Even his beloved Theodosia had left him. She had been shipwrecked, never to be seen again. He wanted to be with her once more. He wanted to hear her laughter and see her charming face light up with happiness. Burr loved her more than anything in his life and longed to be by her side as he remembered. He hoped he would be when this was over.

He looked around the room again. It somehow looked distant. The caretaker of the boarding house was now by his bedside.

But he didn't see her. He only saw the angels.

He let go.

* * *

After the word leaked out of the house that Burr had passed, a well-dressed young man, who had been hanging around the boarding house and who everyone thought was family, stole his way up into Burr's room and quickly made a plaster cast of Burr's face. It was his death mask and was to be shown throughout the centuries to come.

* * *

Connor didn't realize how tired he was until he stepped out of the tiltrotor onto the deck of the aircraft carrier after the hit on the yacht. The weather was calm, and the ship moved quietly through the dark ocean, a silent, moving island. The sound and vibration were like a cat purring in the night. He was always amazed how massive these vessels were, self-contained cities unto themselves.

His eyes had long adjusted to the darkness, as he was on night vision goggles the whole mission. His legs were weary, and he felt drained as never before. He easily made his way to the stairway leading to the bowels of the ship. The adrenaline had left his body, and the letdown made him feel weak after the long, sustained rush of excitement. All of a sudden he was very, very tired. He held on to the railings of the stairs for dear life.

Before entering the passageway, he again looked up at the stars overhead and thought of Kate. He longed to see her. He had not realized how much. His step quickened; she should be already down below. His energy partially returned with the thought of her. A surge of happiness passed through him.

He made his way to the ready room to hear the debriefing of the mission. On the whole as far as he could tell, it was a smashing success. Their objectives had been achieved. The ship was secured and the precious cargo recovered. This included Kate, the data from the computers on board, as well as live prisoners to interrogate and learn more. He stood taller as these thoughts passed through his head.

As he made his way through the myriad of tunnels on board the ship to his destination, he curiously noted a somber look on many of the officers' faces. He had expected a different reaction. They refused to lock eyes with him. Soon Connor rounded the corner to the ready room.

The captain of the carrier met him at the entrance. "Follow me, Mr. Murray," he directed. Connor did as he was told.

They left the ready room and made their way to a small briefing area, one of many for flight crews to prepare individually before their missions. The captain shut the door behind them. The look on his face was grim.

"Connor, I don't know any other way to say this except to just say it." He paused briefly, then continued. "Kate is dead." He let that phrase hang in the air as Connor absorbed its meaning.

"The aircraft in which she was being ferried crashed. There were no survivors."

Connor laughed. He had known this before. It was a dream. *Okay, I can wake up now*, he thought. But nothing changed. This was reality and he knew it. It had happened a second time.

"Not again," he said aloud.

His son screamed at him, "Help me, Daddy!"

Emily screamed, "Connor, I'm burning!"

But Kate was foremost in his mind.

"Be strong, my love," he heard her say.

Connor buried his head in his arms and wept.

* * *

Washington, D.C.
Langley, Virginia

The analysts at the Central Intelligence Agency pored over the treasure trove of documents and data from the raids on Nevis and the yacht. An army of men and women had every resource at their disposal to glean immediate and detailed information from the intelligence captured.

The objective was to acquire the information needed before the markets opened the following Monday. The president did not want to lose his strategic advantage here, so the pressure was on. The task force worked around the clock, decoding computer drives and deciphering reams of paper records.

The main items of interest were the CUSIPs of U.S. Treasury bonds owned by the alliance, now considered the enemy. CUSIP stands for Committee on Uniform Securities Identification Procedures. Every North American financial security can be uniquely identified by an alphanumeric string of characters. This was part of the intelligence recovered from the yacht and from the raid on Nevis.

The United States could be virtually certain who owned each U.S. security at any time based on ownership of the CUSIPs. In other words, the U.S. could identify the owners of its debt piece by piece.

Records of ownership of all bonds outstanding were compiled by the economic task force assembled by the president. With this corroborating data, the team was close to being one hundred percent sure which bonds were owned by the alliance. The ownership was of course layered through multiple offshore accounts and shell companies, all controlled by the member countries themselves.

This and other information was also confirmed by coerced interrogation of prisoners taken from the yacht. The interrogators did not have a lot of time to acquire the information the president needed. This included confirmation of the alliance's economic objectives against the United States and their methods to accomplish these. The interrogations worked, and the information was delivered to Washington.

The president could now act with certain knowledge against his enemies.

* * *

Oval Office

President Walker signed the orders at his desk. The entire National Security staff was there to witness the act. The actions authorized were very dangerous and carried with them many risks. However, so did making acts of war against the United States of America, no matter her weakened condition.

Weakness is risk, the president thought as he attached his signature to the documents. *We will no longer be weak, at least while I am president.* He took no pleasure in these actions, but he also decided he had no choice but to show determination to the world. It was his job to decide if he put America's young men and women in harm's way. He remembered the famous words of Ronald Reagan, "Peace through strength."

The initial orders he signed predeployed forces throughout the world to forward locations so that they would be in position to execute any mission given them. These included naval, air, and ground assets.

He then called the leaders of Congress and invited them to the White House to brief them on the situation. This was required by the War Powers Act. The president had to inform Congress forty-eight hours prior to initiating hostilities with the United States military.

Even though no president considered the limits on presidential power by the War Powers Act valid, they usually complied with the notification requirement.

He asked them to prepare a declaration of war against the members of the alliance and to hold it at bay until his request.

The Chinese military buildup had been reaching a crescendo for years now. They had begun to deploy multiple aircraft carriers in the Pacific Ocean in their quest to achieve a blue-water navy, one that could be effective worldwide in any body of water. They were threatening their neighbors. In fact, they were threatening the world.

The Pacific had been an American lake for decades, since the fall of the Soviet Union. China was intent on changing that.

They resented United States warships being deployed off their coast to bully and intimidate. They especially resented U.S. support of Taiwan. This was their country. How dare another power try to tell them what to do concerning this island.

China also believed they had discovered a way to maintain power as well as make their population happy. They would allow the people to become capitalist—up to a point. Allowing them to become wealthy was a way to keep the Communist Party in power. It was very obvious that central planning did not work. Not even the communists believed in that system anymore. They knew that individuals could allocate capital much more efficiently than any government committee could.

But they were sure to maintain the tentacles of power. Any prospect of unrest or a threat to the power of the Communist Party was swiftly and brutally put down. They did not want any repeat of the Tiananmen Square disaster that had happened in the late twentieth century.

So they quietly built up their military. They persistently stole technology through cyber attacks against Pentagon and civilian contractor systems. They manipulated their currency by keeping it artificially low, which allowed their goods to be cheaper than those of Western counterparts. This fueled a large trade imbalance and built up their foreign currency reserves, with which they bought

United States Treasury bonds. They were the banker to the United States, funding the creation of a vast welfare state in the U.S. that was unsustainable.

Now they held all the cards, or at least enough of them. At least they thought they did.

The question was, which system would win out in the end? Would the boot on the neck of the Chinese people eventually produce significant opposition? Would the people give up political freedom forever in return for limited economic freedom? Or would an economic downturn produce enough frustration that the system could be changed? Or perhaps frustration with the environmental and human rights abuses would do the job.

In any event, China had now forced a confrontation with the United States. This in all likelihood would force all of these questions to the forefront. The United States would finally have to deal with Chinese aggression, and the Chinese people would maybe be forced to decide what type of government they wanted to live under.

* * *

Moscow

Natasha was scared. She had been living a lie for years now. One thing was clear to her. She was a cat with nine lives on her ninth chance. They were onto her. She was convinced of it. There were too many coincidences. Small items in her apartment moved, people following her, faces she saw over and over again in random places.

Yes, they were onto her.

She had to get out. Her handler was right. It was time.

But how?

That remained to be seen. *They will come up with something*, she told herself. She tried to stop herself from panicking.

For now she waited. She did her job as the assistant to the Russian president. Of course this job had many obligations. Any

Russian girl would realize that. And the president was very demanding, downright ravenous, when it came to her. She performed her duties well.

She was from a small village three hours' drive from Moscow, another world from Moscow. Moscow was not really Russia. Life in the village was simple. At the age of seventeen, she had been plucked from the countryside to become a model in the city. She was incredibly beautiful. After that, her life had changed dramatically. That was ten years ago.

She traveled the world. She learned about other countries and other people. She graduated from one of the best universities in Moscow. She was cultured now. She had seen for herself which types of governments worked and which did not.

She was everything the president was looking for. After the relationship started, she was contacted by an old modeling friend. She was turned.

It wasn't that difficult. She had experienced real freedom abroad in other countries. She had seen real democracy. After many late-night conversations with this girl, who happened to work for the Americans, she decided to help.

She was a good listener when not attending to her duties. She passed this all on to the Americans.

She walked down Fifth Avenue like a tourist; how New Yorkers hated tourists. Tourists gawked on the sidewalk and had their faces pointed to the sky. All the while, the locals just wanted to get to work. Inevitably this resulted in a collision. Some poor wife from Missouri gawking at the buildings ran smack into an investment banker in a hurry to get to his office. Coffee was spilled and words exchanged. This was New York after all. Some things never changed.

She kept walking. The guards tried to keep up. Of course the president had Natasha watched and guarded. He could not just let her have her freedom. She was too important to him. In addition, the head of the Security Service had his suspicions.

The president did not believe this. That is why he insisted that she be allowed to accompany him on this trip to the United Nations in New York.

So let her shop, he thought. *Make her happy*. There were benefits to be gained from a happy mistress.

She passed Bergdorf Goodman and crossed the street. She had in mind her real destination, Tiffany's.

The two FSB agents followed her through the front glass doors into the store. The glass cases glittered with diamonds. How the women loved the little blue boxes. There were multiple levels with different items on each floor. The elevator was located at the rear of the building. Natasha headed straight for the lift. She waved to her guards as she entered the elevator to head to the higher floors, where the custom jewelry was.

They let her go. After all, where could she go? What goes up must come down, they thought, and moved their eyes to the front entrance. They would give her some time alone.

Natasha made eye contact with the elevator operator briefly. "What floor, madam?" he asked.

"The top."

He smiled.

The elevator did not stop at the top floor of the store but kept going to the floor below the roof. She quickly exited the lift and sprinted up the stairs to the top of the building. The usual padlock to the roof had been opportunistically removed. The helicopter was landing, blowing her back against the stairway outer wall. Her handler grabbed her arm and pulled her forward. Time was of the essence. Natasha and the faux elevator operator jumped into the aircraft and slammed the doors shut. The pilot pulled pitch on the collective and dove down between the buildings to gain airspeed, and then sped off into the coming night.

She was safe.

CHAPTER NINETEEN

Eastern Europe

The Special Forces teams moved quickly once they were airlifted into position. For the most part they were operating in friendly countries, countries that Russia supplied with gas shipments, shipments via pipeline that is. Most of them were in the former Soviet Union. Getting inserted into the correct position was not as difficult as in Russian territory. Primarily they were flown in, but some were covertly inserted over ground.

The target areas were mostly in Eastern Europe, along the border with Russia. Europe had been weakened substantially by the collapse of the Eurozone and the common currency. Economic growth had been dramatically reduced as budgets crumbled. This left little room for expenditures on military readiness. In fact, this spending had disintegrated. The North Atlantic Treaty Organization was no longer formidable. It still existed but in name only, backed up by American and, to some extent, British military power. Europe had simply relied on American military power for too long and let its own capability atrophy.

The world sensed the weakness. NATO had maintained the balance of power on the continent for decades, but no more. The old European nationalistic fervor began to rear its ugly head again. The economic pain was becoming too great for the populations to bear. The peace that had been kept for decades was unraveling.

The president figured that he had to take the lead here and deal with the international threats to his allies on the continent. They would possibly experience some short-term pain, which would damage their economies even further by his actions. However, the alternative was far worse, as he hoped many remembered from their elders at the beginning of the twentieth century. He hoped they remembered the sacrifices and the suffering endured. They might have to experience them again. The hard lessons might have to be relearned.

Europe had grown soft. They had grown soft on the cradle-to-grave welfare state. Free everything, education, health care, retirement, thirty-five-hour workweek, holidays, et cetera. It was unsustainable. They could not come to grips with that fact.

Someone had to lead.

The main export of the Russian Federation was petroleum products, oil and natural gas. The products were delivered primarily via pipelines into Eastern and Western Europe. The pipelines were numerous and when overlaid onto a map resembled a circuit diagram. When crossing the border from Russia, they created choke points that were highly vulnerable.

America had made great strides in reducing its energy dependence on foreign supplies over the last few years with the development of shale gas deposits throughout the continental United States. She was now the Saudi Arabia of natural gas supplies. America also was now a net exporter of refined petroleum products. The industry was one bright spot in the U.S. economy.

Europe, however, had grown more and more dependent on Russian exports. It was dangerous.

There were multiple direct-action teams inserted into various locations. They each carried the same type of backpack explosive devices. They were also highly trained in how to deploy and use them. The charges were set up in a matter of hours in a manner not to be detected by the naked eye. Primarily they were buried under the pipelines in unpopulated areas. A pipeline was a notoriously hard piece of infrastructure to guard and keep safe. If someone wanted to damage it, they most likely would be successful.

Once the charges were in place, the teams evaded detection and escaped from the area on foot to a designated landing zone. The teams were then exfiltrated twelve hours later by the same CV-22 aircraft that had brought them in.

* * *

Eleuthera, Bahamas

Connor awoke not knowing where he was. The only thing for certain was the horrible feeling in his head. He felt as though his temples were in a vice. His tongue felt like a dry sponge. And he was sweating, way too much.

The Bahamian sun slowly peeked its way through the window into the bedroom, where he lay sleeping on the floor. He was still fully dressed. The geckos began to chirp.

They make such an annoying sound, he decided as consciousness began to return.

He picked himself off the floor clumsily and stumbled into the bathroom to the toilet to relieve himself. He recoiled at the puke strewn all over the floor where he had missed the toilet the night before. Ignoring the smell, Connor drank forever from the sink trying to rehydrate himself. It was no use. Then he made his way to the front door.

He had arrived on the island late the day before. The president had called on the carrier and asked him where he wanted to go. The world was spinning by him. He did not feel part of his surroundings. He let go.

Connor told the president he wanted to go to his beach house on Eleuthera and be alone, so the president made it happen. He flew by helicopter from the USS *Bataan* directly to the island, landing on the road in front of his house. He didn't even remember the flight, just bits and pieces. If the circumstances were not so depressing, he might have been amused.

He had immediately jumped in his truck and drove to the bar where he had met Kate. The memories were vivid. *I miss her.* He felt alone, completely alone. He had called his office and left instructions not to be disturbed for a while. It wouldn't have mattered; the phone had been left at the house on purpose.

The emotional pain was intense. He had allowed himself to get close.

Never again, he vowed.

Maybe it's time to do something different, he thought. He had enough money. Did he need the stress of the markets anymore? The volatility had been crazy the last few years. This was a young man's game.

The question remained unanswered as he stared at the sea. The breaking of the waves along the beach provided a comforting rhythm.

He drank by himself at the bar. The locals knew well enough to leave him alone. They could tell he needed his privacy. Even the bartender kept his distance.

Somehow he made it back to his villa. All he knew was he hadn't driven. The keys were left in his mailbox. His SUV was outside in the driveway.

Somebody took pity on me, he mused.

His head pounded as he made his way out of the house the next morning, but that pain paled in comparison to the sorrow in his heart.

"Tragedy strikes Connor again!" he cynically laughed as he made his way to the beach, tearing off his clothes as he walked. He lowered himself into the water and just floated facedown, occasionally coming up for air. He was oblivious to the world.

* * *

Oval Office

President Walker picked up the phone once the red light started to flash, and he knew he was connected. He knew the Russian president spoke fluent English. He had advantages and disadvantages in this conflict with the Russian Federation. He hoped to play his cards right.

The Russian economy was stagnating. They had not learned the lessons of the Soviet Union's collapse. Although the Russian president was brilliant in allowing the public to have their own lives up to a point, which lessened the tensions and for the most part prevented outbursts of public anger, his government was still controlling the economy from the top down. A few well-placed incarcerations for life as well as the targeted murder of journalists or competitors for power made his point nicely. The people knew where the boundary lay.

Most important industries were under state control. This prevented the creation of new and important technologies. Entrepreneurship was limited by these policies. Corruption was rampant.

Since the severe depression in 2008, the economy had grown very slowly and was highly dependent on energy, wheat, and other commodities. The concurrent global slowdown due to the overreaching of the Western welfare state exacerbated the problem. The Russian president could not afford a slowdown of his energy exports. They were the economy's engine. They were what kept the people happy. They were what kept the peace internally. They were what kept him in power.

The Russian president was ruthless but also a pragmatist. President Walker was depending on this trait.

He listened for a moment and then spoke.

"Mr. President," he began. President Walker was angry. He hoped that anger came through over the phone. "I don't want to play around here. We both know what you have been doing. Please do not try to argue or deny it."

There was silence on the other end, then two words.

"Go on." The accent and the coldness were unmistakable. There was no doubt who was on the other end of the line.

"You have been acting in concert with other countries to inflict damage to the economy of the United States." President Walker waited, but there was no response.

He continued.

"I want you to listen to me clearly. I also can inflict damage against the economy of your country. Yours is a resource-driven system; it is not very diversified. Your main export and the lifeblood of your economy is energy. Most of it is sent through pipelines into Eastern and Western Europe. These pipelines are very vulnerable. I can shut them down for a very long time. I can shut them down permanently. In fact, you need to know that the assets to accomplish this task are in place. All I need to do is make a phone call. Are we clear?"

"Yes, Mr. President, I believe we are," the Russian president answered.

* * *

The designated sites had been targeted for a long time. The Iranian regime had been a thorn in the American side for decades now. From the occupation of the American embassy in Tehran, the Iranians were on a slow but deliberate march to destroy Israel and of course the Great Satan, the United States of America. They had achieved much in this quest. They had asserted themselves throughout the Middle East as a sponsor of terrorism and as a regional military power. They had built an atomic energy program with help from the Russians and others, who were on the verge of giving them a nuclear-armed capability.

The targets on the American military's watch list in-country had long been verified and reverified as conditions changed over the decades.

The president and the intelligence infrastructure felt they had very good information on where in Iran the nuclear materials and facilities were located. The question was really just what weapon to use to destroy them.

Several years before, the Central Intelligence Agency had been very successful in sidelining the centrifuges used to enrich uranium in Iranian possession. They brilliantly inserted a computer virus that caused the devices to spin out of control and destroy themselves. This set the Iranian nuclear program back several years. In fact, the Iranians were still dealing with the lingering effects from the problem.

In addition, the Israeli Mossad had been effective in killing many of the scientists working on the Iranian program. But the program still existed and was very dangerous and close to being successful.

President Walker had made it very clear to the secretary of defense and his general staff. In addition to their military capability, he wanted the Iranian nuclear facilities destroyed completely. He wanted options on how to do this and the probability of success for each.

There were twenty-five nuclear targets in all. All of them were hardened for years deep underground; the bunker walls were said to be sixty feet thick. Conventional weapons had a limited probability of success. The sites were very fortified. However, the president was determined not to leave a nuclear-capable Iran, so he left open the possibility of using tactical nuclear weapons.

He was prepared to use them. They were fairly low tonnage and would be shaped to send the charge deep underground. The sites would be destroyed, and the collateral damage would be minimal. Most of these sites were located away from major population centers anyway. To the president it was an easy choice. Kill or be killed. He had no doubt that as long as Iran was governed by an Islamist regime, bent on destroying the United States and Israel, they would continue to try to harm his country. Threats were no longer appropriate. They had drawn first blood.

There was the issue that the United States had signed a no-first-use treaty against countries that did not possess nuclear weapons. However, he did not care. If he had to use them, he would.

Indeed, he did not want to set a precedent regarding first use, so conventional warheads would be attempted. The United States had been perfecting the art of bunker-buster bombs for decades now. The technology was very advanced. The military had specifically developed conventional weapons for these targets. Each site would be struck multiple times under this method.

He had already moved multiple carrier battle groups into position. In addition, Air Force assets were on alert and being prepositioned as well.

He received the report from the Department of Defense on his options. He chose using conventional weapons against Iran to destroy their nuclear facilities. If they were not effective, then he would have to make another decision for a follow-on attack. Then he knelt down by his desk and said a prayer.

* * *

Washington, D.C.
The White House

President Walker was calm as he sat at his desk in the Oval Office. He was dressed in a dark gray suit with a red power tie. The flags were furled behind him. The lights showed bright. He looked very presidential. The Oval Office setting always gave its owner a sense of power no other competitor could match. It created instant respect. The president was counting on the seriousness of his intentions coming through.

The red light was flashing in front of him to his side, counting down the seconds. The teleprompter was ready. He knew what he was going to say, but his staff insisted on the teleprompter. He wasn't going to use it. His press aide was counting the seconds down and mouthing them. "Three, two, one, go!"

He calmly looked into the camera and waited a few seconds, the suspense building. The networks had been notified thirty minutes earlier he would be making a speech. No one knew what was happening. Reporters were still excitedly streaming into the briefing room.

"My fellow Americans," he said calmly and somberly, "it is my duty to inform you that we have been attacked by a group of international powers. This attack did not come primarily in the form of military aggression, although you know of the Iranian conflict. This attack came in an economic form. There has been a coordinated effort to destroy the United States economy by raising interest rates to an unsustainable level and drive this country further into debt. We believe the Iranian aggression was part of this effort."

The president paused again for effect.

After a few moments he spoke again.

"I consider this economic aggression an act of war."

He let the words sink in.

"This effort was put forth by an alliance of nations, including China, Russia, and the Iranian Islamic regime. There are possibly others involved, but our intelligence has not confirmed those as yet."

The gravity of the situation was starting to hit home. People across the world were mesmerized by the spectacle unfolding.

He continued.

"I have asked Congress to prepare a declaration of war on China, Russia, and the Islamic Republic of Iran. If this aggression continues, the act will be passed into law."

There was a gasp in the room.

"I have ordered the United States Navy to blockade the ports of Iran. I have placed our nuclear forces on DEFCON 3, and I have ordered the United States Air Force to obliterate the military capability of Iran. This is underway as we speak."

They could hear a pin drop, the room was so quiet. Even the reporters were speechless, not even writing in their notebooks.

"Since the action taken against us by China and Russia was not military but economic, I have ordered an economic response."

Again he paused. The silence was deafening.

"I have ordered the United States Treasury to default on the debt owed to all three of these countries. We will not pay the interest or principal on these bonds."

The reporters began texting furiously now on their iPads and smartphones.

"This amount is north of ten trillion U.S. dollars. I have also put our missile defense system on high alert and have given an ultimatum to Russia and China. They will accept these terms peacefully, or I will shut down commerce between our nations and the Western world. Their export-driven economies will starve.

"The path here will be tough; it will be hard. However, maybe Americans will learn to make things again."

"Goodnight and God bless the United States of America."

* * *

Hong Kong

The top floor of the hotel was empty except for the staff and a few guests. It was a luxurious, expansive space comprised mostly of an open conference area. Glass walls all around gave an impressive view of the surrounding territory far below. Chinese artifacts adorned the walls.

They sat at a large, dark, wooden table overlooking Victoria Harbour and the Kowloon Peninsula. Cargo ships and ferries made their way back and forth across the water to either side of the harbor, as they had for centuries. Skyscrapers dotted the landscape as far as the eye could see along the coastline. The city was a mass of steel and humanity. The hotel was one of the tallest on the shoreline, providing a vista to the entire metropolis.

As the men sat at the conference table, they did not notice the view outside; they were focused on the task at hand. Pleasantries were exchanged, and then an awkward silence ensued.

"We moved too soon," the Chinese representative finally said.

"President Walker has been stronger than we expected," said the Russian.

The Chinese man spoke again. "We have been successful in raising the interest rates on America debt. Since the default, they have skyrocketed. We have increased their borrowing due to the conflict in Iran, but we have lost much wealth ourselves. We will now have to slow down our military strategy and rebuild our reserves. What we did not anticipate was the reaction of the American government. Again, I believe we moved too soon. The tiger still has teeth."

"My country requests your help in dealing with the attacks from the Americans," the Iranian minister noted. "We are fighting this battle alone."

"And you will continue to fight it alone," said the Russian. "We will not let ourselves be drawn further into this conflict. We will deny participation in this scheme to the entire world. They will believe us. We will wail and moan about the unfairness of the Americans. How they are using this conflict to default on their debt owed to the world. There will be a sympathetic reaction for all of us," he said.

"We must now fall back and wait for another opportunity," said the Chinese minister. "The Iranians must fend for themselves. Time is on our side. We will be patient and strike again when the time is right, whether it is next week or one hundred years from now. The Americans cannot keep vigilant and strong forever. It is not in their character.

"They cannot now access international markets. They still are spending too much. They have a huge deficit every year, forty percent of their budget. We can still destroy them economically."

He leaned forward and spoke in a low, threatening tone, "We will put pressure on them where they are weak. The weakness is in Europe."

The Chinese minister, when finished speaking, folded his notebook and left the room.

* * *

Major Dan Carter was aware of the existence of the Russian S-300s in Iran. He was not worried. The electronic countermeasures on the B-2 bomber were robust. Only a select few were aware of how effective they were. Plus the plane was basically invisible to radar.

The B-2 program was started in the 1970s. In fact, President Carter found the program so highly promising that he canceled the B-1 program. President Reagan reinstated it a few years later.

Initially designed as a 129-member fleet, the program was so expensive, only twenty-one were produced. At almost a billion dollars a copy, to say the planes are very valuable would be an understatement to the extreme. The aircraft were a national treasure.

The crews had been rehearsing this mission for some time in the simulators. They knew the sequences inside and out. They knew the possible threats they could face during each phase of the mission and how to defeat them. The real thing was almost anticlimactic.

Almost.

His adrenaline was pumping, but he forced himself to be calm and follow his training. Mistakes were made when people were excited.

"This is gonna be a long one," he said to himself as he strapped himself into the cockpit. He adjusted his seat as he liked it so everything he would need was within reach. Then he accessed the checklist and began to turn on the aircraft.

Preflight checks were completed over the next hour, and all systems checked out fine. The time came for the mission to proceed. Final instructions were received from the chain of command. Engines were started. The wheels began to roll.

The *Spirit of Georgia* lifted off from the tarmac of the airfield at her base in Missouri and glided into the air. She was one of fourteen aircraft taking off in flights of two on their way to Iran. It would be a thirty-hour-plus mission, and although normally the B-2 carried a crew of two pilots, there were three on board currently. Therefore they could take turns at the controls while the other slept.

The mission would end up being over forty hours. It was a testament to the stamina of the aircrews, who were highly trained for this task. It was also a testament to the magnificence of the aircraft and all of the other crews that supported her, in the air and on the ground. There were to be multiple refuelings in flight as well as air defense suppression and electronic warfare elements engaged before they arrived in-country.

Each B-2 was carrying two bunker-buster, guided munitions. The thirty-thousand-pound Massive Ordnance Penetrator, or MOP, was designed specifically to destroy deeply buried, hardened targets. That meant that each target would receive at least two rounds. If the first drop didn't destroy the facility, the second or third one would. The most critical targets would receive special attention.

Five more aircraft waited on alert in Missouri and were loaded with nuclear weapons. They were the president's backup plan.

He prayed he wouldn't have to use them, but he couldn't allow a nuclear-armed Iran.

* * *

The first hostile actions taken were a myriad of cruise missile launches from naval and air assets. Over five hundred rounds were fired the first evening. These were aimed at the air defense network and command-and-control systems of Iran. Ten percent of these were targeted at the leadership structure. The country's air defenses had to be degraded in order to ensure air superiority over the target areas. That way, the bomber and ground attack aircraft could act with impunity.

The next phase consisted of concurrent targeting of Iran's nuclear sites as well as energy assets, refineries to be exact. Although the country was awash with oil reserves, their refining capacity was minimal. This was their Achilles' heel. All of the domestic refineries were to be disintegrated. Iran would now be totally dependent on imported refined products.

Therefore, all pipelines leading into Iran were also severed. In addition, the coastline was blockaded by the U.S. Navy. The goal was to bring the economy to its knees by starving the country of energy. This hopefully would lead to a populist revolt to remove the leadership, or what was left of it after the offensive. There had long been a simmering opposition to the clerics and their brutal dictatorial tactics. Now was the time to aid those parties and hopefully bring about a more reasonable government that was friendly to the West.

* * *

Major Carter was back at the controls after a rest period and was tense as they crossed into Iran at high altitude. However, the crew was highly trained and professional. They were also combat-hardened after being involved in multiple conflicts in the Middle East over the last decade. The entry was uneventful. They were feet dry.

It did not take long to reach their initial target and then their follow-on target. Their weapons were released as planned. Now it was up to the intelligence assets to conduct battlefield damage assessments and see if another round of attacks was needed.

"Now it's Miller time," Major Carter said over the intercom to the rest of the crew.

Upon leaving the country and flying over the water again, or feet wet, the crew relaxed somewhat. However, there was still much work to be done. Midair refuelings were a challenging exercise. He forced himself to stay alert and ahead of the airplane. He had to think of what was coming next and be mentally prepared.

The aircraft were not redeployed back to the United States. Instead they flew direct to an unknown forward operating base that was equipped to handle and maintain the B-2. This was a challenge in itself. Specially-equipped facilities were needed to repair the radar-evading skin of the aircraft after each flight. There they rested as the aircraft were rearmed and readied for their next mission.

* * *

Javid Jafari was elated. He had done his job. He believed he was instrumental in leading his country to a different path, a path of democracy and freedom. If he needed to die in this effort, so be it. He was at peace.

He had been educated in the West. He saw the prosperity that their lifestyle and economic system produced. He also was all too aware of the effects of totalitarianism and terror on his people and the pain and suffering it caused. The Iranian Revolution had been perverted. Islam had been perverted. It was a tool to maintain power.

The regime's barbarity was horrific; he could no longer look the other way.

The Persian people yearned to be free. They yearned to be able to return to the success of the distant past when they were a great kingdom and civilization.

That is why he had cooperated with the American CIA when they approached him several years ago to become a spy. Yes, he gave them information and betrayed his government. But in his mind he was happy. He would die with a happy heart.

As an assistant to the supreme leader of Iran, he always knew his location. He always had access to highly sensitive information on the whereabouts of all of Iran's leadership.

He had been passing this information on to his handlers for years now. That is why he was overjoyed when the order had been given to proceed to the hardened bunkers. He went with pleasure. He surmised his time on this earth was almost over.

He didn't hear the bomb coming. He hadn't expected it this early, but he never had time to worry about it. The bunker-buster munitions from Major Carter's B-2 obliterated the complex. Javid died with a smile on his face and peace in his heart.

CHAPTER TWENTY

He hibernated for several weeks at his house on Eleuthera. It was good to be alone. The way the property was laid out to allow him privacy, he would not be seen unless he wanted to be. The small cove in front of his home became his only world, a world he never wanted to leave again.

The locals brought him food from time to time. He was appreciative of that. He had been a good neighbor over the years and had built up some good karma. People were concerned about him.

Time seemed to stand still on the island. The crushing rhythm of the waves brought a comfort, knowledge that this and all things shall pass. His favorite time was dusk, as the sun slowly made its way down, splashing the heavens with Caribbean colors. It was then that he thought of Kate, and of Emily. He knew clearly he was very lucky to have had them both in his life.

He spent many nights staring at the ocean from the deck on his home. The warm summer breeze coming off the water was soothing. And from time to time, he ventured to the bar where he had met Kate; however, the pain there was great and these visits became fewer and fewer. The bartender greeted him as always but left him alone. It was obvious he wanted solitude.

The days passed. He took long walks on the beach. Over time the pain started to recede. Or, at least it became more manageable. He had always been able to compartmentalize things. He would have to do so again. He had to put the pain in a tiny box in his brain and wall it off. It was only to be felt when he could afford to let the feelings out.

There was one thing Connor was having difficulty understanding. Why didn't Burr find the gold? He obviously had been searching for it. The answer remained a mystery.

Eventually he decided to reengage with life and return to Nassau. The decision did not come lightly, but after many days, he knew that was what he wanted. Perhaps civilization would get his energy flowing again. He wanted to revisit the trust. He wanted to solve the riddle about Burr's not finding the gold.

It seemed odd to return to this pirate city. Kate and Alex were dead. The place seemed foreign to him now. The thrill of the hustle and bustle in the streets was gone. He was lonely. He had grown used to not having this feeling with Kate around. It was back. It was back with a vengeance. He was depressed.

He really didn't remember getting to the trust company. He didn't even notice the tourists milling about the shops anymore.

The staff recognized him and let him in. A large Bahamian woman smiled at him and shepherded him to the ornate room to which he had first been shown weeks ago. Nothing in the room had changed. Then they brought him the box, opened it, and left him alone.

My, how far he had come since he first opened the box. *There must be something I am missing*, he thought.

He searched the chest again and again, examining every item thoroughly. Nothing. He had gone through these documents a hundred times. He closed the lid and noticed the golden little lion staring at him. He touched it, caressed the smoothness of the craftsmanship. The gold piece moved slightly as he touched it. *What?*

He pushed down on the golden inlay. The whole lion moved inward. He heard a noise inside the chest and opened it. He had pushed the lining of the top of the chest into the chest itself. He opened the lid so it faced upwards to the ceiling. There he saw a very old parchment pressed to the top that had been hidden inside the lining.

He opened it and began reading.

It was a letter to an unnamed person.

So this was why Burr had never found the gold. He had never found this parchment.

The parchment confirmed what he had found at Hamilton's grave.

Connor left the trust company an hour later after combing the box for any more hidden chambers. There were none.

He had some hope again. Maybe this will all come to some good after all, he thought.

* * *

Hong Kong

The French finance minister entered the executive suite at the top of the hotel where the leaders were located. He was a proud man, an elitist. This task did not come easy for him. How could it? He believed with all of his heart in the European project. He believed in the cradle-to-grave entitlement system. He believed in the state. And most of all, he believed that all Europe needed was to borrow a few trillion euros to buy some more time, and he was sure that Europe itself would work out its problems. He could not fathom failure. It was unthinkable.

He was led to the conference table by a staffer, where the others were waiting. The introductions were friendly enough. However, the pleasantries did not last long.

"Mr. Valentine," the Chinese premier spoke in fluent English. "You have come here seeking our help, have you not? You have a problem. You are out of money. If you are not lent large sums of money, and I'm speaking of trillions of euros, your region will suffer an economic disaster. Have I summed up the situation clearly enough?"

"Yes, Premier Len," the finance minister replied. "I think you have summed up the situation correctly. None of the measures we have put in place over the last decade since the crisis started have been effective. We need large amounts of capital to bail out several economies of the Eurozone and to stabilize our banks. If we are not successful in raising this money, the euro will cease to exist. This would be devastating for all of our economies. If fact, it would be devastating for the world economy." He looked at the men seated around the table and tried to glean their intentions; he was trying to make this their problem as well. "However," he continued, "I do believe with some breathing room the funds will give us, Europe can solve its own problems."

"Seeing as how the United States just defaulted on the money they owe the People's Republic of China, we are very leery of lending you this money. If we would consider doing such a thing, there would be a price. A very high one."

"Premier Len, please outline your terms. Our way of life is at stake, and we do not have many options. I will relay them to my superiors."

"Very well. We require the following. All international transactions by the European Union going forward must be denominated in yuan. U.S. dollar transactions globally will cease to exist. All foreign troops must leave European soil, that is United States forces. NATO must cease to exist. Defense spending in the Eurozone must cease to exist. You must turn over any technologies we deem appropriate to the People's Republic of China. And we expect a reply within forty-eight hours, at which point this offer will be null and void. The Americans have no money. Even though they have defaulted on our debt, they still are indebted to the rest of the world. There will be no discussion of these terms. You are dismissed."

Valentine looked at the Chinese premier across the table, a look of disbelief on his ashen face. *How can I relay this to my superiors?*

The French finance minister stood up and left the room with his tail between his legs.

* * *

Somewhere Over the Continental United States
Aboard Air Force One

President Walker sat in a padded chair on Air Force One. He had asked the staff to empty this part of the aircraft and to leave him in peace. The dull roar of the engines provided a small bit of comfort somehow.

His daughter Elizabeth sat in the seat next to him. There were tears in her eyes, but she did not show any other emotion. He had just told her about Kate's death. She was being strong for him. He knew Elizabeth loved Kate like a sister. She was being forced to face the fact that she was gone.

He looked out the oval window in the fuselage of the Boeing jet at one of the Air Force F-22s flying alongside guarding the president's aircraft. The lines on the fighter jets were graceful, reminiscent of American power. The sunlight glinted off the cockpit glass, and one of the pilots waved at him. He waved back somberly. *How much things have changed over the last few months*, he thought. The world had become a much more disturbing place.

He was playing a game of brinkmanship with the alliance countries. He knew he had to back up any threats he made. He was careful to make sure he could act if his bluff was called. It was a dangerous game, a slippery slope.

It was the financial problems that were killing the country. The entitlement spending was out of control. He had to find a way to bring the country back to fiscal reality and sustainability. That was the challenge. The spending had to be slowed, and the economy had to begin growing again. The debt-issuance cycle to fund further borrowing had to stop. He was fairly new in office, and it was a Herculean task. In addition, the economic downward spiral led to a weakened national security position. It was inviting threats and attacks. He had to shore up America's defenses as well.

He stared back at the aircraft alongside.

"Just don't let her death go to waste," Elizabeth finally said softly. The president was jerked back to reality. "Fix the problems, Dad. Take the hard road and get it done."

President Walker took in the words and pondered them. *Out of the mouths of babes*, he mused.

He would do so. He would take the hard road. *But what does that look like?* he wondered.

***

Isle of Hope
Intracoastal Waterway
Savannah, Georgia

The conspicuously black U.S. government Suburban left the mainland and entered a narrow two-lane causeway that made its way across the marsh, splitting the southern waterway that separated the barrier islands from the Georgia mainland. Their destination was one island in particular. The wetlands separated the island from the neighborhood of Sandfly, an old slave community. Seagulls soared overhead, looking for dinner in concert with the occasional hawk circling above. Connor could see the shells of the creatures that by the billions had mostly formed this man-made thoroughfare littering the sides of the road. He thought of his driveway on Eleuthera in the Bahamas and the shells crunching under his tires as he drove.

The view of the marsh was peaceful, with the reeds gently

blowing in the breeze. The tide was slowly retreating, exposing nests of oyster shells and black muddy banks teeming with crabs. An occasional alligator sunned himself on the salty earth.

It was not a long ride across the marsh and Moon River. Soon they were back on dry land as they arrived on the Isle of Hope. Palm trees greeted them, as well as huge, ancient oak trees dripping with Spanish moss hanging from the branches like a beard. *This is the old country*, thought Connor.

The island got its name from, of all places, the disease malaria. When the aristocracy of Savannah had been smitten with the disease during the colonial period, the residents had fled to the island to escape the sickness, hence the name Isle of Hope.

A quarter mile after accessing the island, the vegetation thickened, and the Suburban turned right onto a wide, tree-lined passageway. The road went on as far as the eye could see. *This is spectacular*, thought Connor. The majestic oaks were welcoming. The branches interlocked overhead and blocked out the sunlight like a jungle canopy. He could imagine a horse-drawn carriage making its way down the lane hundreds of years ago. The view was probably not much different now.

They drove on for what seemed like ten minutes.

Eventually they reached the main structure, which was built in 1828 and still stood in good condition. The state of Georgia had acquired most of the property in 1973, which included 822 acres of a colonial plantation. The original, fortified home had been reduced to ruins.

The Suburban pulled into the turnaround in front of the stately house. Connor stepped out of the vehicle and was followed by a man in his sixties. He was obviously important, hence the multiple bodyguards, who also exited before and after him. They were met by an elderly gentleman.

"Good afternoon, Mr. Secretary," the older man said as he

addressed Connor's companion. "Welcome to Wormsloe Plantation. To what honor do we owe the pleasure of hosting a member of the president's cabinet?"

"Well, Mr. Ulmer, thank you for meeting us here on such short notice," said the United States secretary of the Treasury. "I think Mr. Murray can answer that."

Connor greeted the man and extended his hand for a firm handshake with the caretaker. Then he reached into his jacket pocket and pulled out a sealed plastic envelope. Unzipping the plastic opening, Connor pulled out the old yellowed parchment that he had taken from Burr's chest at the trust. He also retrieved an old iron key. Mr. Ulmer's eyes widened.

"So you've finally come," he said matter-of-factly.

* * *

Several months back, Connor had stood and stared in wonder at Alexander Hamilton's grave at Trinity Church in New York; the large marble tomb with the obelisk on top stood out among all of the other ancient graves. The excitement began to bubble up inside him.

On the bottom right side of the monument, almost hidden by the grass and etched into the marble at the base, was the image of a little lion. It was the same image that was inlaid into the top of the wooden chest from the trust. Below the lion, in block letters was the word "Wormsloe."

Hamilton must have given instructions on his deathbed after the duel to have the etchings made on his grave, Connor thought.

"I know where it is," he said aloud.

* * *

Wormsloe Plantation dated back to the early eighteenth century and had played a role in American history ever since. The property was developed by one of Georgia's original colonial founders, Noble Jones. Although a Tory, Jones fortified the original quarters on the property to guard the intracoastal waterway from Spanish incursion prior to the American Revolution. After his death, his son had inherited the property and been a patriot to the American cause.

The grounds had also played a role in the American Civil War, again protecting the waterway, this time from Northern invasion.

Mr. Ulmer took the parchment from Connor and carefully opened the folded document. A smile broke out on his face as he read the lines of handwritten prose. Connor thought he saw tears in the man's eyes.

"I have waited all of my life for this, as did my father and his father before that." He looked up at Connor and the secretary when he was done reading. He said nothing for a tortured few moments. Then he finally regained his composure and spoke. "Please follow me," he requested politely.

Connor and the secretary with his entourage followed the elderly man silently for several minutes along a trail through the forest along the marsh. The silence was broken only by birds chattering overhead. The moss hung eerily from the branches, and the palms rose from the ground as they got closer to the water. Soon the ruins of the old, fortified home were visible, the tabby walls jutting from the ground in pieces, highlighting the grounds of the old structure.

Finally the old man turned to face them and spoke.

"My ancestors built this property initially to protect the city of Savannah from Spanish invasion. At the beginning of the nineteenth century, my great-great-great-uncle received a visit from another secretary of the Treasury, the first one as a matter of fact. Mr. Alexander Hamilton. It seems that Mr. Hamilton had some items he wanted to store for future use in his business dealings, and wanted the items kept far away from the prying eyes of his contemporaries in New York. So he hired my uncle to store them for him. Here. At Wormsloe. Two hundred and twenty years ago."

Mr. Ulmer held up the parchment for all to see.

"He set up a trust here in Savannah to pay for this storage in perpetuity until the holder of this document returned to claim the items with this key."

He turned again and walked towards the ruins.

Once inside the perimeter of the original house, he made his way to a small structure that one would presume to be a storage shed and opened the lock and swung open the double doors. Inside there was a trap door in the floor, which he opened and at the same time passed out several flashlights, which were mounted on the inside wall.

The party made its way down an old flight of stone stairs into a cellar.

Again, Mr. Ulmer turned to face them.

"Gentlemen, I present you the property of Alexander Hamilton hereby bequeathed to you."

He inserted the key into the lock of the ancient iron door, turned it, and to his amazement, it opened.

Connor pointed his light towards the rear of the cellar and saw trunk after trunk lining the walls of the underground space. There must have been one hundred of them. He walked to the closest one and carefully unlocked the lid. It was filled with gold bars.

* * *

Office of the Secretary of the Treasury
Washington, D.C.

Connor looked around the office and noticed the personal mementoes of the man he was speaking with. He had picked up this habit in his early business training, and it served him well. What a person put in his office told one many things. It also provided items

219

for conversation. The Treasury secretary was speaking. Connor forced himself to rejoin the conversation.

"The law of the state of Georgia gives the treasure to the beneficiary of the trust," said the secretary. "Officially, the gold is yours. That is how Hamilton designed it. It was taken from Latin America but we do not know where. The Bahamas could have a claim, as it was taken from there as well years later, but there is the small fact that they do not know about it. However, I believe Hamilton had an ulterior motive in mind. I believe he thought that whoever was privy to the information inside the trust would be selected with the highest of standards. I believe he wanted the gold to belong to the United States of America."

"I believe that as well," said Connor.

"We are prepared to offer you a finder's fee, if you are prepared to turn over the gold to the United States Treasury." The secretary paused for effect. "Your country needs your service, Mr. Murray," he said rather matter-of-factly. "We are prepared to offer you a finder's fee of ten million dollars." He let the words sink in.

Connor's mouth was open but he was unable to speak.

"And I should make other points known," he continued. "We will be prepared to fight you in court for the rest of your natural life if you do not agree. We believe this gold belongs to the people of the United States."

"I agree to your terms, Mr. Secretary," replied Connor. "The gold is yours, as it should be."

* * *

Oval Office

The northwest door, which gave access to the main corridor of the West Wing, opened slowly. President Walker rose and walked around his desk. He had been told she was entering the office but had no idea what she looked like.

Natasha walked in.

President Walker was stunned by her beauty. She had to be late twenties, very slim and fit, with long, black hair. It was a natural beauty, not enhanced, not overdone, a Russian princess from long ago.

Wow, he thought. The Russian president has good taste.

He walked up to her and extended his hand.

"Natasha, I want to extend to you the heartfelt thanks from the people of the United States. Your efforts on our behalf have been invaluable. We are in your debt. I know you have been through an extremely stressful situation and need some time to yourself. Please know that I and my staff are at your service. Let us know what we can do for you."

She smiled a genuine smile, and her face lit up.

"Mr. President, it is an honor to meet you," she said in fluent English, although with a strong Russian accent. "I have my reasons for helping you, which we can discuss at some point if you would like. However, I have always dreamed of seeing California. I have heard so much about it. I love architecture and want to see the bridges, museums, everything. Maybe when it is safe, I can spend some time there. Perhaps, aahh, how do you say in English, I can be a tourist?"

"Done," said the president.

"It would be good to relax and enjoy myself!"

He laughed. "We have to debrief you first. You are going to spend a bit of time in seclusion with our team, but I will honor your request."

She smiled again. "Thank you, Mr. President," she said, and was led from the room.

CHAPTER TWENTY-ONE

The Corner of Wall and Broad, New York City

It was a ceremony of sorts, a kind of testament to the courageous and forward-thinking actions of a man several hundred years before. It was a tribute to his service to his country.

Connor walked slowly down Broad Street in front of the New York Stock Exchange. The J.P. Morgan building was on his right, the House of Morgan. Here, the United States had been saved, rescued by this banker decades before during another financial crisis. John Pierpont Morgan used millions of his own money to stop the financial panic of 1907.

At the time, the charter of the Bank of the United States had been allowed by President Andrew Jackson to lapse before the Civil War. Therefore there had been no central bank that could act as a lender of last resort. When the federal government couldn't act, Morgan did. Convincing other tycoons to put up money with his own, he staved off a crisis. His legacy still exists today in the form of J.P. Morgan Chase, Morgan Stanley, and others. The crisis also gave weight again to Hamilton's idea of a Bank of the United States. This eventually became the Federal Reserve Bank of the United States.

Much had happened in this small corner of real estate. Connor gazed at the impressive smooth stone blocks that comprised the building. "The Corner," as it was called, was intimidating. *It was probably designed that way*, he thought.

A large bomb had detonated here in September of 1920. The pockmarks in the granite slabs of the building were still visible to the naked eye. The perpetrators had never been identified, and the event had further inflamed the Red Scare that was sweeping the country. The area was deep with history.

The Treasury secretary walked beside him. They both wore long coats, as winter was approaching. It was an unusually cold morning for this part of the year.

They turned left at Wall Street. The street got its name from its origin as the northern wall of New Amsterdam, the original city on Manhattan Island. The wall kept the Indians out of the settlement. Traders would gather here under a buttonwood tree hundreds of years ago to exchange goods and eventually shares of companies. Eventually they formalized the trading process. This was the beginning of the New York Stock Exchange.

The two men soon passed the Bank of New York on their left. They stopped and turned to face it. Alexander Hamilton had built this bank. It was his baby, in addition to the Bank of the United States, the Coast Guard, and many other pillars of American society.

After a moment of silence, they turned and continued down Wall Street to Trinity Church. The street was blocked off by the police to give them security. They could now roam the area freely. They passed through the entrance and then through the gate to the cemetery on the south side. They continued to Hamilton's grave, where Connor had stood months before.

The secretary spoke as they faced the grave.

"Secretary Hamilton, we are here today to thank you for your efforts on behalf of your country. They have endured over the centuries and are helping us immensely today. Your gold has been returned to the United States Treasury at a time of great need. I assure you that the wealth will be used with the utmost of care and frugality. Thank you again."

"Thank you, Secretary Hamilton," Connor added as the events of the last few months flashed through his mind. Snow began to fall.

They left the cemetery and headed back to the waiting limousine.

* * *

"So how do we get out of this mess?" Connor asked the secretary as they were whisked back to Midtown Manhattan on their way to JFK airport. The police escort made the usual thirty-minute drive much shorter. It was the kind of interference that New Yorkers hated in their daily lives. Connor winced as he saw the pedestrians not being able to cross the road due to police barricades. Many times he had cursed the occupants of vehicles like the one he was in now.

The secretary didn't answer right away. He just shook his head in disgust.

Finally he said, "Well one thing for sure is it's not gonna be easy. We have dug ourselves a giant hole. We have to get the economy growing, for one thing. We can pay off our debts if we unleash the American people. We have to get government off their backs and allow them to do what the American people have always done—innovate and make money.

"And we must have sound economic policies. Many of the imbalances of the past few decades are starting to be unwound through whatever means. The American economy is very resilient. We are changing from an energy importer to exporter. We must further that process. Although our defaulting on our debt to the Chinese was undesirable, it was necessary. The president was right to do so. We will achieve peace only through strength, not weakness. The reduction in interest expense will give us some breathing room to build up our defenses again.

"We must reform entitlements. They are killing us. Reducing

spending and reforming our entitlement culture are priorities. It doesn't work. It hasn't ever worked. Even the communists know that. Look at China, Russia, Vietnam. The list goes on and on. They are capitalists now. We have here the greatest economic and political experiment in human history, and we are blowing it. Unbelievable actually."

They sat in silence.

"What about the currency?" Connor finally asked.

"If we can do all the things I mentioned, the dollar will take care of itself. With your trillion-dollar find, I believe there is enough gold to return to the gold standard. We have to peg the currency to something of value. Right now, the paper is worthless. Relying on fiat money opens the door to central banks printing money to pay off debts. It allows for massive government spending, keeping the current government in power. However, in the long run, it only brings economic misery in the form of inflation and loss of purchasing power, a lower standard of living for everyone. We have to base our currency off our hard work and economic and fiscal discipline and something of value. Then we will be okay."

Connor looked out the window as they passed the Empire State Building. He marveled at this monument to America's financial strength in the past, and he wondered if the country still had the fortitude to make itself strong again.

* * *

The Oval Office

He felt cold. It was a strange feeling. It was plenty warm inside, as winter was approaching and the staff had raised the indoor temperature. But he still felt cold. President Walker glanced at the bust of Churchill that had been returned to the White House by the British after an absence. It was placed prominently in his office. Perhaps he was feeling what Churchill must have felt, staring down the Third Reich. It was a chilling experience. He tried to draw strength from those who had sat here before him.

The European Monetary Union was gone. The euro had collapsed. The Europeans were now conducting transactions in yuan. NATO was finished. To save itself, Europe—with the exception of England—had given in to Chinese demands. *The special relationship still existed after all*, he thought. Australia was also still with him, in addition to Israel. It was as if the old British Empire held together against the mysterious Asian world.

What was he to do? What should he tell the American people? Of course, they would survive, but the world was very different now, much more dangerous. Sacrifice would be the name of the game going forward. That is what he had to tell the American people. He had to be honest with them about where they stood, where they stood together. He would be strong and would rally the people to the occasion. *Just as we have done many times before*, he thought. *This is no different.*

Yes, he would be strong for them. He shivered with the cold.

EPILOGUE

Connor walked along the beach barefoot as the warm water from the waves repeatedly bathed his feet. The bright Bahamian sun beat down on him, and he could feel his shoulders and the back of his neck burning.

Time to put on more sunscreen, he thought.

It was several months since Kate's funeral. President Walker had been there. Everyone who knew Connor was sympathetic, but there was really nothing anyone could say. However, he felt the funeral was for Kate, not him. It was for her family. He was amazed at the amount of people who showed up. She was a special person. Her family bore the real loss.

He had known Kate for only a few weeks, but she had touched his heart. Now his heart was empty again.

He had resigned his position at the firm. He didn't need the stress anymore. He needed to clear his head, and he wanted to simplify his life.

All was not lost. He had been awarded the $10 million finder's fee for the gold from the U.S. Treasury. Hell, he was rich. And his country was safe, for the time being. But he had lost two dear friends. He had to believe Alex at heart was a friend, even though he'd had his own agendas.

Funny how life can change in a New York minute. Life's a box of chocolates.

The BlackBerry in his pocket vibrated. He pulled it out. It was a 202 number coming in. He didn't recognize it. He answered the call.

"Mr. Murray, it's the White House calling. The president would like to speak to you. Please hold."

Connor stopped walking and looked up at the sky. It was a beautiful day. A few small white clouds were drifting aimlessly across the blue background.

"Connor, hello, it's President Walker. Look, I was just wondering how you are doing. How are you handling things? You are in the Bahamas, I understand?"

"Yes, sir, I am," said Connor. "I'm making do, just clearing my head. Spending a lot of time on the beach."

"Well, good to hear. Let me know if I can help you with anything. Call my chief of staff for anything, all right?"

"Thank you, sir."

"Oh and one more thing," said the president. "There's someone I want you to meet. I know it's kind of early, but I think you would like her. You two seem very much alike."

"Really? You're playing matchmaker now, sir?"

"Yes, maybe I am. And by the way, Connor, I have to tell you one thing about her. She's Russian."

ABOUT THE AUTHOR

L Todd Wood is a graduate of the U.S. Air Force Academy, an aeronautical engineer, an Air Force pilot, and a former international bond trader with expertise in conducting business in over forty countries. He is a national security columnist for *The Washington Times* and editor-in-chief of Tsarizm.com. Follow Wood on Twitter at @LToddWood and on Facebook at facebook.com/LToddWood/.